MW01613468

ONE NIGHT IN WAIKIKI

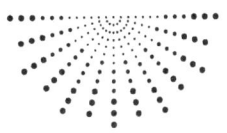

DREA BRADDOCK

Copyright © 2021 Drea Braddock
All rights reserved.

To my SWO
You support my dreams before I even dare
to dream them, push me to be better,
and make everything more fun.
Love you forever.

1

FERN

I shouldn't have listened to Brooklyn about the dress. She's shorter than I am and much more comfortable showing off her body. I planned on buying something flirty and fun once we got to Honolulu but they're ready to hit the town now. I guess I can't blame them. The trip, transiting from San Diego to O'ahu, was not important enough to warrant permission for excess speed so we crawled through the Pacific Ocean for a week.

By the time the ship docked at Pearl Harbor we were all beyond ready for liberty call (the beginning of shore leave on dry land) and the chance to get off the floating tin can we call work and sometimes home. I tug at the tight, lacy black minidress, feeling exposed. This is so much more skin than I'm used to showing. I've been messing with it since we left the ship.

"Stop fidgeting, Fern!" Brooklyn commands as she slides into the rented convertible. "You look hot, own it!" Emily pats my hand good-naturedly.

Saturday evening Honolulu traffic sucks as much as San Diego's, maybe worse. I'm sure having a shitload of ships from all over the world here for the next six weeks isn't helping either. That's the only reason we're here, after all. RIMPAC, the Rim of the Pacific Exercise, is the largest international maritime warfare exercise. We're not thinking about that though. For tonight, we're just three single women on a gorgeous tropical island, ready to let loose and have fun.

"What should we do first? Drink, food or fun?" Emily basically shouts from the backseat.

"ALREADY ON IT!" Brooklyn yells back. Of course she has a plan. Brooklyn is our resident party planner. She is all about the nightlife and probably scoped out everything exciting within walking distance from the hotel weeks ago. We check into our room and she only allows us to drop our bags at the foot of the bed before she's marching out the door, leaving us tottering behind her. Or maybe that's just me doing the tottering. I don't go out much and as a Naval Surface Warfare Officer (or SWO, rhymes with whoa) stationed on a Destroyer, I don't have a lot of opportunities to wear heels.

"I feel ridiculous!" My voice is whinier than I intended but I stand by the sentiment. None of this is me. I don't strut down the street in sky high heels. I don't wear skin-tight dresses. I don't spend my nights off in bars. I'm more likely to be described as a homebody, or quiet, possibly boring. I'm considering claiming a headache and going back to the hotel room for a long bath and binge watching Netflix when I run right into Brooklyn. She is stopped in the middle of the sidewalk, in a power stance, legs wide and hands on her hips. Her brown eyes are narrowed at me.

"I told you she'd do this," she addresses Emily.

"Do what?" I cross my arms over my chest, irritation bubbling up.

"What you always do. Find a reason to ditch us and hang out alone. I think you might be incapable of having fun!"

"What? I am not!" I sputter. "What's this about ditching you? All I said was I feel ridiculous. I look like a weird Club Hopping Barbie version of myself! I'm nervous about flashing everybody!"

2

"That's how it starts." Brooklyn narrows her eyes at me. "You complain about how you look or how you feel and then you make some excuse and leave. I found this cute little karaoke bar and we were going to drink and sing silly songs and enjoy our first night in Honolulu. I had this perfect vision of the three of us, like the beginning of a hilarious joke: a blonde, a brunette and a redhead walk into a bar...but no, Fern has to ruin it. I should have known you'd never let your hair down with us."

Brooklyn is right, I do usually make excuses to hang out by myself on our days off. I'm an introvert and I share a state room with 2 very extroverted women. Sometimes a girl needs some time to herself to recharge! But, there's one little problem.

I hate being told who I am.

HATE.

IT.

I may be a quiet, somewhat goofy girl but woe be to you if you try to put me in a box. I'm serious. Like, I have a tattoo that has absolutely no real meaning to me, simply because of this personality flaw. I had something put on my body, *permanently*, to prove a point after being told "someone like me" would never get a tattoo. Was it mature? Nope. But my brain was all "fuck you! I do what I want! You don't get to decide what type of person I am!" I joined a ROTC program because an athlete-asshole-bro type guy gave me the once over with his Judgey McJudgerson eyes and declared that chicks like me couldn't hack it in the military. Well, that and the whole it-paid-for-college thing. But I initially looked into it because he said I couldn't do it. I'm in the Navy now, suck it!

I backpedal, pretending I wasn't looking for an out. "I'm in! I never said I wasn't. I need a little reassurance, I guess. Can I pull this off or do I look like a faker who is trying too hard?" Because they're ultimately supportive and kinder than I deserve, Brooklyn and Emily assess me, dropping the argument. Emily runs her fingers through my hair, arranging

3

it around my shoulders. She's our resident nurturer, forever mothering us. My scalp is still a bit tight from wearing it up in a bun all day.

"Your hair looks great and your makeup is perfect. You have nothing to worry about. If I had your porcelain complexion I would save so much money on makeup! Buck up, Fernie!" She gives me one last fluff and pats my shoulder. Emily steps back and Brooklyn takes her place. The petite brunette stalks in a circle around me, making me feel like I'm her prey.

"I don't know what you're worried about. I told you before, you look hot. As long as you act like you believe that, you'll be golden. Now, enough of this. Let's get some drinks, pick some kick ass songs, and become the queens of karaoke! Ground rules: no work talk! No last names! Girl code!" We bump fists and enter the bar, side by side, Brooklyn's hand covering the sticker on the glass that reads, "Sounds gay. I'm in!"

The inside of the bar is kitschy in a really fun, bright way. There are splashes of vivid color everywhere and the decor has an Asian flare. There's a bright rainbow neon sign, hanging on the back wall, that reads "Aroha Beaches." It makes me snort. Only a bar called Wang Chung's could get away with that joke! The place is filled with music and laughter and, given the number of ships converging on Oʻahu, probably a good number of sailors. We don't mix work and dating. Good thing it's pretty easy to spot a military man. And the majority of the guys here probably aren't looking at us for company. This may be ok after all! We divide and conquer: Emily snags us a table, Brooklyn goes to ask about the song list, and I order the first round of drinks. The bartender on my end sort of looks like the human version of a hot anime character. It could be an effect of the black lights and neon but his smile is legit dazzling. I bet he rakes in the tips.

"What's the best cocktail you make?" I have to raise my voice to be heard over the guy singing Bon Jovi.

4

He eyes me carefully. "You want the *Rough Turbulence*. Spiced rum, dark rum, our housemate ginger beer, bitters and lime. Plus, it looks good in photos."

"3 please!" I give him my card for the tab and Emily waves at me from a tall table across the room.

"I'll bring them over." I tuck my card back into my purse and he shoots me that dazzling smile with a wink. Yep. He makes bank. I make my way over to our booth, conscious of how the dress is riding up the back of my thighs with every step. I'm not going to complain though. I don't want Brooklyn to be right about me.

"Em and I are going to do Britney Spears. I hope you don't mind. We always do it together, we've practiced the choreography from the music video!"

I have to laugh. "Of course you have. I can't wait. I'll cheer you on!" Mr. Smile brings over our drinks as they rush over to check where they are in the order. I can't believe they're going to sing and do choreography in front of all of these people stone cold sober.

"You're not joining them?" He spins and skillfully places a glass at each spot, coaster and cocktail napkin in place, before turning back to face me.

"I'm more of an 80's girl. Plus, they do this together all the time. They're a twosome."

"First time?" I nod nervously. "Oh, we've got something special in store for you then! We love newbies here! Do you trust me?"

"No! I don't even know you!" I giggle, taking a sip of my drink. "Oooh, this is delicious though! It's definitely giving you some points."

"Sweet. You can trust me, you know. I won't steer you wrong. You're going to sing, but I'll give you enough time to drink that first. I'm Adam, by the way."

"Fern." I shake his hand, then immediately wonder if you're supposed to shake hands with the bartender. That was probably too business-like for a party girl on the town. Too

5

late now. It's gotta be obvious that I don't know how to play this role anyway.

"Alrighty, Fern. Let me know if you ladies need anything and keep an ear out for your name. There's no stage, you're given the mic and sing wherever you want." I'm going to need another one of these if I have to get up and make a fool of myself all alone. The opening bars of "Toxic" ring out and people start howling. The crowd is actually awesome. Everyone is having fun and no one is heckling. Emily and Brooklyn are singing with enough enthusiasm to cover their lack of skill and their dancing is completely over the top. They're working the room, moving up and down the aisle. I love it. I'm cheering along with everyone else, egging them on. When the song ends, they return to our table, glistening from their exertions and laughing.

"You guys killed it! I feel sorry for that little dude who has to follow you. I'll be right back, I'm going to get another drink." Adam sees me coming and leans against the bar, waiting. "Can I get a rum and coke?"

"What kind of rum do you like, Fern?"

"Black rum. Anything local I should try?"

"I have just the thing." He grabs a glass, his movements like a graceful dance. "Just so you know, the guy at my twelve o'clock has been watching you since you came in. Not in a creepy stalker way. He's yummy and very oblivious to my flirting. I wasted some of my best material!" His self-deprecating grin is even better than the tip-grabbing-smile from earlier. I prefer genuineness. "Use the mirror." He ticks his head slightly to indicate the mirrored wall behind him and I carefully look through the crowd. Sure enough, over my left shoulder, a guy is watching me intently. A really, really hot guy.

"Yummy is 100% the right description. You're sure he was looking at me though? Maybe I happened to be in his line of sight."

"Nope, definitely watching you. Even when your friends were dancing through the aisles he sat facing you. Swoon!" He hands me my drink. "Don't forget, you'll be up soon." He moves down to the next customer and I make my way back to our table, trying not to look at the hot blond. I flick my gaze over towards his table and catch his eye. The brief connection makes me feel like I just dropped down the first valley on a rollercoaster, fear and exhilaration holding hands. Emily and Brooklyn are talking animatedly when I slide back into my seat.

"Fern! Don't be obvious but scope the guy at the bar—tall, dark hair, really nice feet. Girl code: I saw him first, I think we're vibing. He's definitely not gay. I'm going to talk to him." I sneak a peek over my shoulder. He is good looking. The foot thing seems like a weird detail, but I'm not judging.

"I'm going in!" Brooklyn stands up, drink in hand, and walks over to the bar. She has a natural sensuality that I envy. Of course the guy immediately notices her, she's gorgeous. She subtly flicks her long dark hair over her shoulder and leans in to speak to him, lightly touching his forearm. I'm in awe as he angles his body towards her and signals the female bartender to get Brooklyn another drink. *How does she do that?* I have no idea how this works.

"Why did she even tell me about the guy?" I ask Emily.

"Girl code." Her brown eyes scan the crowd as she sips her *Rough Turbulence*.

"What does that even mean?"

"Basically it means don't hit on a guy she's interested in. Brooklyn tends to get what she wants and we wouldn't want to compete with her anyway."

"Gotcha." I hear Adam's voice amplified and look up to see him stepping out from behind the bar, microphone in hand.

"Aloha! We have a treat for you tonight! It's time to pop a cherry!" Everyone starts cheering loudly. "Fern! Come over here. This is Fern's first time doing karaoke, friends! Let's give her a warm welcome!" My cheeks burn and I'm silently praying that I make it through the crowd without falling on my face. I arrive without incident and there's more cheering, the loudest being from my friends. "And since you can't lose your virginity alone, my new friend Fern is going to be singing a duet!" He looks down at the paper in his hand but I can see there's nothing written on it. What is he up to? "Deacon, come here and treat my girl Fern reaaaaaaal good." One corner of his lips quirk up and he hands me the mic. My apparent admirer, the tall blond hottie, grabs the microphone next to me as the music starts. My stomach settles as I recognize the song. That's one less thing to stress about. He starts singing "Don't You Want Me" by The Human League in a sexy baritone and I sway to the music, taking the opportunity to watch him.

He really is delicious. And safe. I don't date guys from work. Guys on the ship are either off-limits (fraternization rules means no dating enlisted guys), too much like my brothers, or plain ol' jerks. I don't need the complications. I've learned my lesson there. Deacon has a bit of a beard and the top of his golden hair is longer and wavy. There's nothing military regulation about him. Watching him keeps me from worrying about all of the eyes that are on me. He's maintaining eye contact while he sings and his smile makes me feel all melty inside like the nachos I heard the table next to us talking about. I like that he knows the words to this classic 80's jam! I almost miss when I'm supposed to come in because I'm locked onto him.

I join him on the chorus, just in time, and I can hear Adam catcalling from the bar. When my verse starts I try to let myself be two-drinks-in Fern and loosen up. I can sing, so that part isn't terrible, but I'm not performer material. I only have to get through the rest of the song. Thankfully most people are drinking and interacting with those around them and not staring at us. That makes it easier. I can feel the beat vibrating in my chest as I sway my hips. It feels awkward but I'm trying. Deacon is treating it like a private show. He hasn't looked at or acknowledged the bar full of people once. His attention is as intoxicating as Adam's strong cocktails. He reaches out, sliding his hand down my arm. There's an energy in his touch. If making me feel like the only person in the crowded room and undressing me with his eyes is a seduction move, it is 100% working. We finish the song, embarrassingly close, and I become aware again that we have an audience. The crowd goes wild, more from being kind than because of our performance, and Deacon takes my hand, guiding me towards his seat. I'm in the chair next to him before I can even process or protest.

"My drink is at my table." I stutter, suddenly awkward again.

"You already finished it." I look over and see my empty glass.

"Huh. I guess I did." His lips curve up, perfect teeth flashing, and I go weak at the knees. I didn't even know that happened in real life. Whoa. His smile could give Adam's some serious competition.

"Do you want the same thing?" I nod dumbly and he gets up, handing our microphones over and going to the bar. I'm still blinking slowly, watching him cross to the bar, when Emily and Brooklyn rush over.

"Holy shit! He is hot and super into you!" Brooklyn grabs my hand and gives herself a high five with it.

Emily drops my purse on the table, always taking care of me. "Nice, Fernie! I filmed the whole song because that was the cutest thing ever! I'll send it to you!" Emily absentmindedly braids her light blonde hair, leaving it hanging loosely over her shoulder.

"Quick, before he comes back!" Brooklyn brings our heads together in a huddle. "I may leave here with James, just

9

FYI." She's studying me as if I'm a specimen under a microscope and it makes me feel squirmy. "It doesn't really matter though. We all know you're not the one night stand type and Em hasn't found anyone yet. You'll both be back in our room regardless. I'll see you tonight or in the morning." Her tone isn't rude but it gets my hackles up. There she goes again, telling me who I am. She gives me a quick squeeze and goes back to the dark haired guy who is apparently into her enough to ask her to his room. Not that I'm surprised. Brooklyn is a closer.

Emily shoots me a thumbs up and a smile, sauntering over to the back corner of the bar and leaving me alone. My nervousness is battling that fiery resolve to prove everyone wrong. I don't have time to decide what I'm going to do though. Deacon is back, placing a glass on the tall counter in front of me.

"Black rum and coke, right?" His fingers brush mine, sending goosebumps up my bare arm.

"Yes, thanks. What are you drinking?"

"Bourbon and coke, actually."

"Is it good? I don't know a lot about alcohol. I only ordered a rum and coke because I know I don't dislike black rum." He slides his glass towards me, pointing at it with his chin. I take a sip, absurdly aware that his lips were just on this glass. The soda is cold and sweet and the bourbon whiskey traces a warm path to my belly. They compliment each other perfectly. Delicious. He takes the glass from my hand and the way his eyes are taking me in makes it obvious that it was merely an excuse to touch again. It gives me a thrill. "I like that! I think that may be my new drink."

"Do you live here?" His voice is low and soothing with faint traces of an accent I can't place. Something Southern-ish.

"San Diego. You?"

"I just moved here for work. I don't even have a place to

live yet although the maid service in a hotel room is a nice perk."

"Are you staying close by?"

"Over yonder." He gestures with his head in the general direction we walked from. I don't know why I asked, basically it's all hotels down here. I wish they taught Normal Conversation 101 in school!

"What do you do?" I find myself leaning forward as we're talking, wanting to be closer to him. Away from the neon lights I can see that his eyes are a bright green and his hair is shades of golden brown and blond. He's distractingly good looking. Way out of my league. Normally I might have noticed him the way one notices a work of art, but I wouldn't have considered approaching him. No way.

"I'm a dentist." He stretches his hand out and stops mine before it reaches my face. I hadn't even realized I was moving it in front of my mouth. It was an automatic reaction. "Don't do that. Please?"

"What was I doing?" His fingertips are tracing along the edge of my hand. The contact has my pulse racing.

"Whenever I tell someone I'm a dentist they try to cover their mouth with their hand or stop smiling with their teeth. You don't need to do that. You have a beautiful smile." I laugh, unable to keep my mouth closed. "Why are you laughing? I'm qualified to say that! It is my *professional* opinion that you have a beautiful smile."

"I do try to take good care of my teeth, but I had an ex who called me Snaggletooth. My front teeth overlap a little and I never had braces so I don't have the picture perfect smile that you have."

"Perks of the job. Who wants to see a dentist that doesn't have a perfect smile? You know what's less cool? Having braces in college. The ladies love a grown man with braces."

I roll my eyes. "Right. I'm sure you really struggled with the ladies." He laughs and I fall a teensy bit in love with the sound. It's so genuine and warm.

11

"I was a late bloomer, Fern. You tell me: how am I doing?"

Adam appears at my elbow with a glass of ice water. "Yeah, Fern, how is Deacon doing? He already popped your cherry. Any other items he can," he places the tip of his tongue on his upper lip suggestively, "help you scratch off your list?"

I purse my lips at him, narrowing my eyes. "You're trouble, Adam. It's true though, it has been a night for new experiences. Thanks for the water, I needed it! Cut me off. In fact, I'd like to close my tab."

"Yeah, you want to make decisions with a clear head." His eyes flick over to Deacon, about as subtle as a sidewalk sign spinner. "The blonde said to tell you she's going back to the room and the brunette left with the guy with nice feet. I'll bring your check." Great. They forced me to come and then ditched me here without a room key. I quickly forget my dilemma though. Deacon's eyes are on mine and I can't look away. There are flecks of lighter green in his irises, like sun on summer grass. I'm still watching him, the look feeling every bit as intimate as his touch, when Adam brings me the check to sign. He earned his big tip.

A guy is singing "Adore You" skillfully a few feet away from us and it's the nudge I need. I love this song and I can be spontaneous. I *can* be fun. I rise to my feet and crook my finger at Deacon, beckoning him to join me. He steps close enough that I can feel the heat from his body on my skin. His hand slides down my back, pulling me closer still, our hips swaying to the beat. My eyes are level with his lips. Soft pink flesh catches between his teeth and the air hitches in my lungs. I can smell the whiskey on his breath and the warm, leather undertones of his cologne. He's caressing my back, fingers almost brushing my ass with every pass. He brings his face down and I can feel the warmth of his exhalations on my cheek. I don't know if he's going to kiss me, if I should want him to, or if I'm reading too much into this. I'm so out of my element but my body is on high alert.

I'm the girl that always does the right thing. The girl that spends her weekends at home, alone. The girl who plays it safe. And all I want to do is pretend to be someone bolder, freer, braver. Just for tonight. I run my hands up his chest, over his broad shoulders, and around his neck. Lifting up on the balls of my feet, I press my body closer and touch my lips to his. I feel like a lightbulb being placed in a live fixture, suddenly and unexpectedly glowing to life. He holds me tight and his stubble lightly scratches my face as he angles his for more contact. Soft lips touch almost delicately until the tip of his tongue slips out. It's electric. I want more but he pulls away, cupping my face with his hands and staring deeply into my eyes. He places a firm kiss on my lips and I feel it tracing a path like the whiskey, this time the warmth pooling between my legs.

"I'm not one for making out in public. Can we go back to my room?"

"Yes." No thought. No hesitation.

He grabs my purse, lacing his fingers through mine and leading us out the door. Adam throws me a shaka from behind the bar and I can't help but grin. I speed up my steps to keep up with Deacon's longer stride. My nerves are buzzing. He leads us into the same hotel we left earlier! As soon as we enter the hotel I start to panic. I don't know how to do this! What happens when we get to his room? Do we talk? Is there a getting comfortable period? Shit. This was going so well and I'm about to make it weird and awkward. There's no avoiding it. It's what I always do, in every situation. It's like a super power. I make things awkward. I never know what I'm supposed to say. I don't know what to do with my hands. I fidget and stumble over my own words and my skin is so pale that all I have to do is think about blushing and I become a glowing beacon of embarrassment. The elevator doors close and my heart is racing. I can feel my fingers starting to shake. I open my mouth, probably to say something embarrassing before my brain catches up with my mouth, and Deacon's

13

thumb glides over the vein on the inside of my wrist. He caresses slowly, bringing my heart rate down and I audibly sigh instead of speaking. He's like a weirdo whisperer. Those jeweled green eyes gaze into mine, easing my nervousness.

"I've got you."

2

DEACON

This is so unlike me but I have no intention of stopping. Not tonight. Not with her. I'm a serial, casual dater but I've never slept with a stranger. I haven't been able to take my eyes off of her since the moment she walked into the bar though. I slipped the overly happy bartender a twenty to add me to her karaoke song. I don't want to think about what is smart or what is proper. And now that I've gotten a taste of her, I can't. Fern is an intoxicating combination of bold and unsure. Her pulse beats wildly in her wrist and she seems nervous. Yet, she kissed me first. That's genuinely never happened to me before. I always take the lead. It's definitely a turn on being wanted like that.

I open the door to my room, grateful for my decision to leave on a lamp earlier. The door falls closed behind us and I don't have to leave her alone for even one moment. Her mossy green eyes are wide and she's pulling down on the bottom of her dress. I still her fingers, running my hand over the smooth skin of her thigh. She exhales shakily and I claim her mouth, letting my hands explore the curves of her body. Her lips are satiny, sliding under mine, and she tastes sweet. Kissing her is everything I imagined it would be and more. She places her hands on my chest and pushes me against the wall. Her palms slide down my torso, fingers slipping up inside my shirt and splaying across my stomach. I clench automatically when she shifts closer, her hip pressing into my growing erection. She hasn't stopped kissing me, our tongues dancing as her fingertips playfully stroke nearer to my waistband. I groan against her, skating my fingers from her delicate collarbone down over the hard peaks of her nipples. Her head falls back, eyelids fluttering, exposing the creamy white column of her neck. It's a target I can't resist. My lips and tongue trace up her throat, her skin blushing and pulse racing. I reach her ear and she jerks backward, covering her mouth to stifle a nervous giggle.

"Sorry." Her cheeks flush a deeper pink and she's nibbles her bottom lip. "I hate having my ears kissed."

"Avoid the ears. Gotcha."

"As long as I'm making embarrassing confessions, you should know this dress is all I'm wearing." The rhythm of her speech speeds up and she gestures with her hands but my brain is frozen on what she revealed, on what can be revealed with one swift motion. "It's not mine and my friend is smaller than I am. It was too tight for underwear and my boobs are so small anyway a bra wasn't even necessary..."

"Fern," I interrupt her. "Where's the embarrassing confession? I'm struggling to figure out how you telling me there's only this tiny black dress between me and your bare skin is anything but the hottest fucking thing I've ever heard."

"You say that but I could look like a bog troll under here." Her little pointed chin is quivering slightly and I can feel the waves of anxiety coming off of her even as she smiles. Emotional drama like this ranks high on my reasons to avoid relationships. You don't have to navigate the landmines of a woman's fucked up self image if she's not relying on you. I sound like an asshole, even to me.

"I'm going to need you to stop talking now." I run the pad of my finger over her lip, tugging it from the grip of her teeth.

"I've never done this before. I'm getting the sense you haven't either. But I want you. What do you need?"

"I don't know. Unless being super awkward is a turn on. I've got that on lock down."

"Everything you do works for me, Fern."

She starts unbuttoning my shirt with shaky fingers, the light touches on my skin setting me on fire. There's heat in her gaze. Those glimpses of uncertainty should not be such a turn on. What is wrong with me?

"Shit. I wasn't expecting you to look like this." She runs her fingers over my chest and down my abs. Suddenly the hours I spend at the gym every week are more than worth it. "What else are you working with, Deacon?" She's a little bolder now. It's hot. My shirt drops to the floor, shorts following quickly, and my dick is straining to escape my briefs. "I'm gonna be honest, I've never been a fan of tighty-whities but *day-um*! I guess I didn't realize how sexy they could be." Her voice is soft, the joking hitting me harder because of the note of wonder in her voice. God help me but I want to impress her. I still get a rush from being seen and desired instead of laughed at. I try to shrug my shoulders and act like I'm not internally doing a happy dance. I definitely didn't get dressed tonight thinking someone would be coming back with me.

"It's hot here. The less I can wear, the better."

"I agree. Less clothing is better. Lose 'em." I have no problem complying and seeing her reaction to me naked makes me harder still. She runs her tongue over that full, rosy lower lip, desire in her eyes. The feeling is very mutual.

"Please tell me you have a condom?"

"I told you, Fern, I've got you." I slide the thin black straps off her shoulders, pushing her dress down to her waist to reveal perfect, rosy nipples begging for my mouth. Who am I to deny them?

"I don't know what the fuck you're talking about. Your boobs are too small for what? These things are perfect." She shudders underneath me as I suck one pink peak into my mouth. I release it, moving to the other and her skin pebbles everywhere my tongue touches. She runs her fingers through my hair and I kiss a path down her torso, pushing her dress down as I go. Every inch of her is small and delicate, surprising given her height. Once the black lace clears the swell of her hips it pools on the floor at her feet. She steps out of it and her shoes. I'm facing a whole new world of pale skin and a small patch of red curls. Before I can touch her she steps back, walking further into the room until she reaches the bed. I stalk after her, reveling in the hungry way she's watching me. Her thighs hit the edge of the mattress and she scoots towards the middle of the bed. Her green eyes never leave mine. She's so effortlessly sexy. When I reach her she lies back. Her long red hair fans out, dark against the white bedding. I'm aching to touch and taste every inch of her.

"Fucking hell. How did you end up here with me?"

"I'm asking myself the same thing. Are we sure you're real?" She pinches me and I jump, making her giggle. "Get down here."

Sliding my hands up her legs, I make room for myself until I'm able to lie flat on the mattress with her thighs over my shoulders. One swipe of my tongue and she's lifting off the bed. I want more. More of her taste, more of her reactions, more of those soft little sounds she's making. She lets out a long, faint moan, feet flexing against my back. Her muscles tighten and she shudders beneath my tongue as I taste her again and again, driving her higher. She pulls at my hair but I'm not stopping until she comes.

"I want you" she gasps, her voice breathy, "it doesn't have to be...I want," I growl against her sensitive nub and she doesn't finish the thought. I double my efforts and her hips rise up to meet my mouth. "Ohhhh," she cries out, her pitch rising until her voice breaks, her body tightening as her center pulses under my tongue. Once she relaxes back into the bed I kiss my way up her body. Fuck, she feels incredible.

"You're so soft," I whisper, my lips brushing her skin. Our mouths meet in a tangle of tongues and nipping teeth. Wet heat is sliding against my cock and it's taking all of my willpower not to push up into her like this. I clumsily reach for the drawer of the bedside table where I stashed a box of wishful thinking condoms. Thank you past Deacon for dreaming big.

"I don't think I can yet," she whispers, eyes half-open. "Everything feels so sensitive and I've never..." she stops talking, watching me roll the condom on, her eyes widening almost comically. Everything she feels is immediately projected over her face. I bet she's a terrible liar.

"Trust me?" I prop myself over her, keeping my eyes on her. She nods, biting her lip and I join us together. I push in slowly and her mouth tightens the smallest bit.

"I've never been able to..." she whispers and I glide out and back in slowly. Instead of grimacing and staying tight, she relaxes with the lighter thrust. That's good. The last thing I want is Fern feeling anything but pleasure. I keep a gentle, easy rhythm and she sighs, "oh, fuck, that's good." No kidding. Good doesn't even begin to cover it. Her hands clutch at my back and she wraps her legs around me. I don't want this to end too quickly but every move, every sound, every touch is pushing me higher. She pulls my face down until our bodies are pressed together, sweat making our movements slide, as she licks a line up my neck and bites at the corded tendons. That's my perfect pleasure button and she pressed it on her own, without me saying a word. I groan, increasing the pace, the tension building.

"You can't do that unless you want this to be over. It feels too good."

"All of this does. I don't know how much more I can take. I'm either going to have another orgasm or die."

"First one. Let's do the first one. Come with me, Fern." She arches her back, pushing up into me and I thrust harder. She's tightening around me and my release is right there, like

19

lightning about to crack across the sky. She squeezes tighter still and I break, growling again and crashing into her, all control lost. She's clutching me, biting into my shoulder and panting as her body shudders through the aftershocks. I roll onto my back, trying to catch my breath before I can get up to get rid of the condom. I stumble into the bathroom, goosebumps erupting on my skin in the blast of the air conditioner. She hasn't moved when I come back and I want to freeze the image in my mind. She's the most beautiful thing I've ever seen. How can she not see that?

I slide next to her, kissing up her neck, steering clear of her ticklish ear, and making my way back to her mouth. I could lie here, only kissing her, for the rest of the night. Maybe longer. It really is too bad she lives in San Diego. I wonder if I could see her again, before she leaves? Fern traces her fingers over my face, sighing into my lips.

"Thank you, Deacon."

"I've never had that reaction before!" I laugh, caught off guard.

"I find that hard to believe. I feel like I should be sending you a thank you card!"

"For sex?"

"For *that* sex, yes! I've never had two orgasms before." She blushes prettily. "I thought I couldn't because I'm too sensitive. It was...uncomfortable when I tried in the past. You paid attention to me in ways I didn't even know were possible. I didn't know I could feel like that."

"Well, in that case, you're welcome. Any time. I am at your service. I could make it my mission to make you feel like that." I wink at her and she laughs, the sound light and melodic. I prop up on my elbow, unable to stop touching her soft skin. "I don't think I've ever seen a redhead without a million freckles. I hate to keep using this word, but your skin is perfect."

"I take my sun protection very seriously. If I even think about the sun I get burned." She pauses, as if she's debating

20

something, before changing the subject. "You said you just moved here, did you leave anyone behind?"

"Nope. My last girlfriend didn't like the direction I wanted to take my life. She wanted to put down roots, have babies, live next door to her mother. I wanted to travel more, see the world a bit before I settle down. I'm focusing on work and having fun right now. Last I heard she's well on her way to her dream, pregnant and living behind that picket fence in Louisville. What about you? You're not a cheater, are you? Probably should have had a proper conversation before."

"No! Never. There's no one. I'm not very good at dating. I'm socially awkward and selfish, too introverted and very busy. There's not a lot of room for a boyfriend in my life right now." She keeps running her hands across my skin. I'm glad I'm not the only one that wants to stay connected right now.

"My bullshit detector is going off, Fern. From where I am you're gorgeous, funny and one time with you definitely wasn't enough." I rub myself against her unsubtly, ready to go again. She pushes me playfully and I pull her against me, kissing her until we're both lost again. I lose my bearings a bit every time her lips meet mine. Is that normal? I've never experienced it before.

She pulls away. "Deacon. I should probably go."

"Why? I wasn't really pushing for more sex. I'd like to keep kissing you, though."

"That's not it! I don't really want to stop kissing you but I'm starving! I haven't had dinner, just 3 drinks, and after the workout you gave me, I need food. My stomach is eating itself."

"Then let's go eat. Would you have dinner with me? There's a restaurant downstairs."

"Are you asking me out?" She props herself up on my chest, looking me in the eyes.

"Was that not clear?" I run my hand down her back. I can't stop touching her.

"Are you sure you want to take me to dinner *after* you got sex?"

"Hey! I'm offended. I would never ask a woman out for dinner to get sex!" I'm smiling and the conversation feels like banter but, if she was serious, I think I would actually be offended.

"I don't get the vibe that you're like that. But there's not really any reward for taking me out."

"Being with you and eating is the reward, Fern. I'd want to do that regardless of what we just did." Her responding smile is sweet enough to cause a cavity. She leans down and kisses me. Her touch is light, not hungry. It's the end of a conversation instead of an invitation for more.

"Well, ok. I think we've gone about this ass backwards but yes, let's go eat."

She slips back into her dress and it's hard not to think about how she looked without it. I pull my shorts on and she eyes me, tongue running along her bottom lip again.

"You're going commando?" Her voice is husky. It seems I affect her as much as she affects me. I grin at her in answer, buttoning my shirt. "That's mean. How am I going to focus on dinner?"

"The same way I will while knowing you're naked under that dress: with great difficulty."

It's late enough that we're seated immediately. There's live music over in the corner, far enough away that it's in the background, a pleasant soundtrack to our evening that doesn't prevent conversation. Over burgers and fries we trade stories about growing up in Virginia (her) and Kentucky (me), how unreal and beautiful Hawai'i is and how delicious fries are. We spend a lot of time on the fries. I don't think I could be with a girl that was anti-potato. Carbs are a gift. I'm beginning to see why she says she's awkward but I think it's cute. She gets a little flustered and trips over her words when she's excited, but she's smart and funny. The waiter asks if we want dessert and she subtly bounces in her seat, eyes shining. I don't think she even knows she's doing it.

"Which dessert do you want, Fern?" That sweet smile of hers gets me. Fucking adorable. She orders and I'm surprised how quickly the dessert comes out. There really wasn't any wait. Do they have plates of prepared desserts sitting around? The waiter brings back a big slice of lilikoi cheesecake, sitting the plate in front of her.

"Scoot over here and share with me." She hands me a fork and gestures to the open space next to her. I slide my chair over until our legs are touching. Her knee is pressing into my thigh and it's not enough contact. I rest my palm on her leg, skating along her silky thigh until my fingers can slip beneath her dress. She scoops up a bite of cheesecake, her eyes never leaving mine. I move my hand higher, teasing us both. I'm interrupted by a loud cracking noise and Fern yelps. *Did that noise come from her mouth?* She drops her fork, the clatter of flatware against the glass of the plate startling. The waiter is running towards us and she leans forward, spitting a giant diamond ring onto the plate along with partially chewed cheesecake and blood.

"Miss, I'm so sorry, I brought you the wrong plate!" The waiter is babbling and Fern is holding a napkin in her mouth, eyes watering.

"I think I cracked my tooth!" I grab her chin, trying to tilt her head back and she slaps my hand away.

"Let me look, it's my job!"

"For the love of God don't look in my mouth! This is already humiliating enough!" She's mumbling around the sodden napkin, blood and saliva creeping down the dampening paper. A young guy jogs over, frantically running his hands through his hair.

"Was that my cheesecake? Is the ring ok? I knew I should have given it to her myself! Who wants jewelry that's been in their dessert?" A woman steps up behind him, shrieking and bouncing.

"You were proposing? Ethan, yes! YES!" She stops jumping up and down and wrinkles her nose at Fern. "Gross! Why is there blood on my ring?" I glare at the waiter and the chaos he's brought with him.

"Get them out of here. Take this plate. Send the manager. Now." My voice is steely and he gives me a frightened nod before scurrying away.

"Fern, please let me look at your mouth." She shakes her head again, a tear running down her cheek. The waiter is back, following tentatively behind an authoritative looking woman with a severe haircut. She apologizes and offers us another free dessert. Fern tries to talk and I interrupt her.

"Don't talk until I can get a look at that tooth."

"I wanna go. Can we go?" She mumbles around the napkin.

I turn to the manager, angry and feeling strangely protective. "We appreciate the offer but she probably broke her tooth on someone else's engagement ring. Clearly she's not going to be eating anything. And of course we're not paying for that dessert. That's not even a kind gesture at this point. We would like to pay and leave. I'll make sure you get the bill if she ends up needing emergency dental services." Suddenly our meal is free and they're ushering us out with more apologies.

In the elevator I'm finally able to wipe the tears from her cheeks. I pull her to my chest, wrapping my arms around her and resting my head on hers. Can I do this? Are you supposed to hold and comfort a one night stand? I'm probably crossing a line here but I'm not an asshole. I can't push her out the door. And what's more, I don't want to, even if it goes against my own rules. I guide her into my room and she relents, allowing me to check her teeth. Another tear traces along her nose.

"Did I hurt you?"

"No. I'm just so embarrassed. Shit like this is why I don't

date. I'm a disaster." I shine my phone light into her mouth, inspecting her molars and the surrounding area.

"That wasn't your fault. I shouldn't have distracted you and our waiter should have been paying attention. It could have happened to anyone." She winces as I gently pull her chin down, opening her mouth wider.. "You have a cut on your gums and you may have cracked a filling. It's hard to tell in these conditions. It's not an emergency though. You'll be ok to wait and see your regular dentist." I'm not sure what to do now. She looks up at me, a small teardrop dropping off the end of her eyelashes.

"This might be awkward but, would you mind if I stayed? I don't have a key to my room and I texted Emily but she never responded. She's a really deep sleeper. Like, dead to the world kind of sleeper. I'm pretty sure this isn't how this is supposed to work but," she twists her fingers together, twining and untwining them nervously, "I'm also not ready to leave." I should keep my distance, do my best not to blur the lines any more, but I do the exact opposite. I cup her face in my hands and kiss her softly, worried about hurting her.

"I wasn't going to push you out the door, Fern. I'm not ready for you to leave either. Would you be more comfortable if I slept on the floor?"

"Don't be a dumbass. It doesn't suit you." I bark out a surprised laugh. "We already had sex, what's the point of creating arbitrary boundaries now?"

"So we'll sleep together. I prefer that."

"Um, Deacon?" I raise my eyebrows. "I don't have anything but this dress, as I'm sure you recall."

"Excellent. I'll sleep naked too. In solidarity. I don't want you to feel singled out." She tilts her head, raising an eyebrow at me. "Or," I amend sheepishly, "I can give you something to sleep in."

"You're a good host. You don't happen to have face wash, do you?"

"I do, actually. Don't look so shocked! Just because I'm a

25

guy doesn't mean I can't take care of my skin!" Her lips are twisted and she looks like she's trying not to laugh. "Ok. Fine. Full disclosure: my sister bought it for me. She said washing my face with a bar of soap is criminally stupid."

We wash our faces with the grapefruit scented cleanser Daisy bought me and brush our teeth. Fern is very careful, wincing. Little Miss Always Prepared wasn't wearing underwear but she does carry a travel toothbrush in her purse. As a dentist, I find that very attractive. She leans against the bathroom counter, watching me as I put my stuff back into my shaving kit.

"You'll have to thank your sister for me and my sensitive skin! Oh wait. Don't do that. How would that even work? *This random chick who picked me up at a karaoke bar appreciated the face wash!* Maybe don't mention me at all."

"You think you picked me up? How's that, exactly?"

"I got you to dance with me. I kissed you. Those are pretty big things! Especially for me! I paved the way."

"I can see that. I thought both moves were incredibly sexy. But you're wrong." She scoffs and I want to kiss the scowl right off of her face. "You were mine from the moment you walked in that bar, Fern. I saw you and I was done. I wasn't going to let anyone else so much as talk to you. *Mine.*" I punctuate the word with a kiss that leaves her clutching at my shirt. "I paid the bartender to let me sing with you. I bought you a drink and took you to my table. I asked you to leave with me. I'm claiming victory on this one."

"I've never been picked up before. I liked it. Good job."

"I've never been kissed first before. It was awesome. It made me like you even more." Her smile is like a gold medal. She walks back into the main room, strips out of her dress, and hangs it on the back of a chair.

"Did I tell you how gorgeous you are? I've had the thought so many times but I can't recall if I've said it out loud. I've never been affected by someone so quickly and completely. You bowled me over with one look." She blushes but doesn't move to cover herself up. She simply stands there, letting me look at her. The looking makes me want to do a lot more than that and my body makes that pretty obvious.

She clears her throat and squares her shoulders. "Something to think about while you're getting naked: I want to have sex again. With you. Obviously. It's ok if you don't want to because of my mouth, but I thought you should know."

How am I supposed to respond to a statement like that? Was I going to say no? I take her to bed. This time it's gentle and slow. Fern makes me want to be tender. I'm savoring every second, trying not to think about what happens next. Definitely avoiding addressing what I want to happen next. I never do more than this. Never get closer than a date or two. I fall asleep with her tucked up against me and wake up to an empty bed. I shouldn't be disappointed. I mean, what did I really think was going to happen? We'd be pen pals and see each other on video chats? She said it was a one night stand. I guess I can admit now that part of me was hoping she'd change her mind.

❀

3

FERN

I hate slipping away while Deacon is still asleep but it's
necessary. I woke up wrapped in his arms, his chest warm
against my back. How much I want to stay there freaks me
out. I need to get back to my own room before I build it up
into something it's not and break my own dumb heart. This is
why I'm not a one night stand kind of girl. I can't separate my
emotions. I feel too much and I get attached. Even now, as I'm
grabbing my phone and shoes, I can't help but stare at him
one last time. I wish I could run my fingers through his golden
waves and rub my cheek against the scratchy stubble
darkening his jaw. He looks like the muse for a Roman
sculptor, from the straight line of his nose leading to his
kissable lips down to his hard, muscular body with the sheet
pooling at his waist. It's all begging to be cast in marble for
eternity. I sneak a photo, as much to remind myself that this
actually happened as to remember how he looked, and I let
myself out.

I only have to go up two floors to get to my room. I knock
softly on the door and it opens almost immediately. Emily may
sleep like the dead but she's also a very early riser. Brooklyn is
standing behind her, still dressed in last night's dress, looking
like she just got in.

"You slut!" She screeches, throwing her arms around me in an exuberant hug. "I didn't think you had it in you! Please tell me you came from the blond fox's room?"

"I did. Did you just get back too?"

"Yes! James was dreamy! I'm seeing him again tonight. But who cares about that, we want the tea!" They drag me over to the bed and Emily, ever the caretaker, makes us each a cup of coffee. I don't share everything; I want parts of last night to be only mine. They sigh at the right parts and laugh at my embarrassing moments. Telling them about how Deacon treated me makes it all feel less like something I dreamed.

"So when do you see him next?" Emily asks, sipping her own coffee.

"I don't. I don't have his number. I don't even know his last name." They both stare at me blankly until my cheeks are as warm as the cup in my hands.

"But you said he was sweet and sexy and went all alpha on the restaurant manager! Why wouldn't you want to see him again?" My stomach knots up and I tighten my fingers around the recycled cardboard cup, soaking up the heat.

"I thought that was what I was supposed to do! That was my first time—I followed your rules! We're only going to be here for six weeks and you know me, I'll just end up falling in love with someone that saw me as a vacation fuck! I'm incapable of casual."

"That's not a flaw." Emily smooths my hair back soothingly. "You're not a surface person. You go deep. You're a feeler. We love that about you."

Brooklyn shakes her head. "Oh, Fern." Their sad, exasperated expressions are making me feel even more like I made a mistake. Like *I'm* a mistake. I can't take it. I need to get out of here before I cry and humiliate myself.

"I'm going to shower and then I have plans to see a friend from Norfolk."

I hurry through my morning routine, suddenly anxious to

get out of the hotel before I run into Deacon. I stand by my reasoning. I could already feel myself getting attached. I don't think I was wrong, but I wish things could have gone differently. Seeing him would be embarrassing after I snuck out. I pack my gear, order a ride share, and head to pick up the motorcycle I rented.

It's probably seated in the same part of my personality that hates to be told what I can and can't do, but I love subverting people's expectations. I may be 5'9" but I'm often referred to as "cute" or "delicate." I've even gotten petite before even though it's clearly not true. People think that I'm younger than I am, weaker than I am, and assume I work with kids or cuddly animals. I'm gleeful when they find out I'm an officer in the Navy who loves kickboxing and riding motorcycles. Brooklyn has the car, I can ride with her when I need to, but I plan on getting around Oʻahu solo on a Harley. It's already hot, but I put on my riding gear: armored pants, boots, gloves and a jacket with plating. There's always an element of danger for motorcyclists, and I'm not going to make it worse by getting out on the highway without a helmet and protective clothing. My mama didn't raise morons.

Slipping through the traffic is a rush. The roar of the engine, the vibration of the bike underneath me, the blur of cars as I fly around them — it's one of my preferred highs. I take the highway that cuts across the middle of the island, going through the Koʻolau Mountains. I had been told about the beauty of the drive, but hearing about it didn't prepare me for the view coming out of the long tunnel that cuts through the mountains. The highway is raised high above a basin of valley. Everything is a lush green and the ocean is like a sparkling turquoise and blue jewel all the way to the horizon. The colors are almost too beautiful to be real. This is, hands down, the best ride I've ever taken. I follow the curves of the road down until I'm in the shadow of the deeply creviced mountains, heading into Kaneohe. Bluetooth in my helmet tells me where to turn and I cruise through crowded older

houses, then busy businesses and back past homes. The
residential street takes me closer to Kaneohe Bay, edged with
tall palm trees, its surface carved by sailboats. I've barely
parked, shaking my hair out of my helmet, when my friend
comes running to greet me.

I've always considered myself slightly taller than average
but Norah has almost a half a foot on me. She's more than six
feet of blonde perfection: miles long legs, ridiculously toned
body, sexy pixie cut and she's seriously hilarious too. She's so
badass! If I didn't know her I'd be as green with envy as her
spring grass eyes. Sometimes I still am. My first sea tour would
have been a train wreck if it weren't for our friendship. She
kept me sane.

"You're here!" She pulls me into a hug. "I'm so excited
that we'll get to hang out this summer! Come in the house.
You can change or whatever and I thought we'd go get
breakfast." She introduces me to her housemates. Ames and
Jay are stupid hot, but my body doesn't react at all. Deacon
may have ruined me. Ames is even my type: charming, sexy as
hell Southern accent, tall and built, basically looks like a
human Ken doll and yet, nothing. If anything, his voice makes
me think of talking with Deacon over dinner and the cute way
he referred to the "hollers" in the hills of "Kentuckiana."
Ugh. It's good that I left. It was one night, not a relationship!

I leave my gear and change into a comfortable sundress
and sandals. It's barely 8 am and the temperature is already
nearing 90, the air dense and moist. The back of my neck
feels damp under the weight of my hair and I hastily pull it up
on our way out to Norah's car.

We catch up over spam fried rice with over-easy eggs. We
linger, talking, which makes it easier for me to baby my
mouth. Norah has only been on island a couple of weeks. In
that time, though, she's found roommates to share a house
with a view of Kaneohe Bay and has found a friend in her
neighbor, a Navy wife and mom. I'm envious of that for sure.
I could never forge relationships that quickly. In San Diego I

have Brooklyn and Emily but, as much as I like them, I know our friendship is one of convenience. We work together and live together because none of us has anyone else in California. I can't imagine either of them working to stay in touch once we get our next set of orders, though. They both possess a social ease that has them collecting people in their circle wherever we go.

I've never been very good at making friends. The few friendships I've ever had tend to be like what I have with Norah: a friendly extrovert adopted me and I cling desperately, usually driving them away with my neediness. Norah has always had a lot of other people in her life but she was my only friend in Virginia.

The rest of Sunday passes in easy, relaxed camaraderie. I hang out with Norah and her housemates and am treated to her baking. Man, did I miss Norah's cupcakes! I savor it, and not only because my mouth is tender and aching in time with my pulse. She repeats that I'm welcome to stay in the extra bed there any time I want. I might take them up on it. Waikiki is fun, but a real house, with genuine people that could potentially be friends, on the windward side is more my jam. I'm looking forward to liberty now. I may actually get to see more of the island than the harbor and surrounding ocean! I'm a little sad to say goodbye and head back to Pearl Harbor.

Liberty ends at 5 am tomorrow and then we roll into our regular work week, RIMPAC sea exercises and 6-section duty to stand watch. Brooklyn and Emily let me know they're spending one more night at the hotel but I decide to go back to the ship. Another night in an adult-sized bed would be nice, don't get me wrong, but I'm still nervous about running into Deacon. Or worse, going to look for him. I know which room is his and I'm not sure, if I'm sleeping two floors up, I'll have the self-control not to knock on his door and invite myself back into his bed. It's safer to check in early and avoid the crush of sailors trying to get back onboard tomorrow morning. I'm not a coward. I'm being responsible.

I almost believe it too.

I check in and go immediately to our state room to get some ibuprofen. My mouth, which had been at a dull ache all day, has ratcheted up with a throbbing heat. It hurts to chew on that side and the pain is now radiating up into the rest of my face. I sleep restlessly and wake exhausted. It's fun that something so small can create so much trouble. Or not. It's the worst.

I make it through khaki call — the morning meeting between the officers and chiefs before the day starts — wishing the Executive Officer would hurry up and speak faster. There are so many *piggyback on thats* and *oh, by the ways* and *to tack on to what she saids* and I'm losing my mind. I'm not an impatient person, normally, but I'm hurting and crabby. Finally, four thousand years later, I'm able to go to the nearest dental clinic on base.

The wait isn't terrible but, again, I'm in pain and struggling to be pleasant. I fidget in the dental chair, tapping my combat boots and drumming my fingers on the arm rest. The door behind me opens and a smooth voice, warm like Kentucky bourbon says "I'm Dr. Coleman. It says here you may have a cracked filling?" I'm frozen, jaw gaping open, mouth pain be damned, unable to answer. What kind of prank is the universe pulling right now? The golden waves are trimmed to regulation length and combed in place, the stubble is gone, and holy fucking hell there are sexy tortoiseshell glasses perched on his nose. Somehow he's even hotter than he was on Saturday, and when his emerald eyes look up from his notes and meet mine, I audibly squeak like a cartoon mouse.

"Fern?"

"Dr. Coleman." I find my voice and then it gets away from me, like a stream flowing down a mountain, picking up speed and volume as it goes. "You're a Navy dentist, because of course you are. This is what I get for listening to my stupid friends and avoiding personal details. I thought I had already reached peak embarrassment this weekend, but I should have

33

known better, this is me we're talking about. There's always room for growth." I drop my head into my hands, groaning.

"Take a breath, Fern." I peek through my fingers at him, and he appears to be struggling with what to say. Apparently only one of us suffers from verbal vomit. "You're in uniform. So…you're not on vacation. I thought you said you live in San Diego?" I don't want him to think I'm a liar. I didn't tell him I'm in the Navy but, to be fair, he never asked about my job.

"I do. I'm here for RIMPAC. I'm the Force Protection Officer on the USS DECATUR. I took liberty this weekend since I didn't have duty."

"I'm sorry, I'm trying to wrap my head around this. I never would have pegged you as a sailor. And when you snuck out without a note or exchanging numbers or anything, I thought I'd never see you again, because that was the way *you* wanted it." There's hurt in his eyes and I hate that it's there because of me, but it's hard to focus on that at the moment.

"Deacon, I don't *not* want to talk to you but, do you think you could help me with the reason I'm here? I'm in a lot of pain right now."

"Shit! Sorry. Let me get a closer look at that tooth."

This is awkward. I'll admit, I had been entertaining fantasies of seeing him again, when I wasn't actively trying not to think about him, but never like this. This sucks. The lowered light is painfully bright, even against my closed eyes.

"Your filling is definitely cracked." A dental assistant comes into the room. "I should have pressed for you to get it taken care of on Saturday. This is my fault." The tech is smiling at Deacon like he invented teeth whitening. I hate her immediately, and the surge of jealousy catches me off guard, making me feel guilty. Her eyes narrow on his hand, which is resting on my shoulder, and he stands up abruptly. "Lacey here is going to take you down to get a quick x-ray. I want to make sure the roots aren't damaged and we'll go from there." Now that we have an audience, he's Dr. Coleman again.

Once he has the images of my teeth, I'm back in the chair,

tapping and drumming. My anxiety is growing with every passing moment. I've never been freaked out by the dentist before but everything that has been left unsaid between us is eating at me. I don't know if I'll be able to fix things or if Deacon even wants to talk to me again. Should I want to talk to him? Is it dumb and selfish to want more than I already got? Why can't I be satisfied, as is? This is the worst possible time to be obsessing over things I can't control.

"Hmm," Deacon's glasses slide down his nose and he nudges them back up with his knuckle. Now that I think about it, I remember him doing that at the bar. I thought it was a nervous tic, but it must be an unconscious gesture because he usually wears glasses. It's cute. Like, fucking adorable. "Your teeth look good, it's only that old filling that's broken. I'd feel better if we go ahead and replace it now." He turns to look at me and I jolt, trying not to look like I was staring at him. The corner of his mouth quirks up. Busted. "Are you afraid of needles, Fern?" His eyes flick over to Lacey. "I mean, Lieutenant Junior Grade…" he has to consult his notes again, "McClellan? Of course it's McClellan. I mean, look at you." I giggle and Lacey seems to be mentally stabbing me. Yikes. This chick is going to have her hands in my mouth in a second?

"Needles are fine." Lacey fetches whatever he's asking for but I'm not really listening; I'm watching him work. He has a calming presence, as soothing as his voice. He's good at his job. Lacey pries my mouth open, none too gently, and I keep my eyes on Deacon through the prick and cold sting of whatever they use to numb me.

"We'll give that 10 minutes to start working and then get started. Be back in a few." Deacon leaves but Lacey stays, a pleasant smile on her face with dead eyes like a great white shark. For the first five minutes, she hums along with the music, smacking her gum and ignoring me. I idly check my phone, happy to be ignored. I may linger over the photo of Deacon sleeping. Yummy indeed. Lacey changes tactics.

"You two seemed awfully familiar. Strange considering this is his first day. How do you know Dr. Coleman?" She's fishing and I don't like playing mind games. It pisses me off.

It's not easy to talk around the weird mouth opener thing with a partially numb mouth but I manage quite nicely, if I do say so myself. "You mean besides the sex?" She chokes on her gum and is bent over, hands on her knees, coughing when Deacon comes back.

"Everything ok in here?"

She narrows her eyes at me but stands up, flashing her fake smile. "All good."

"I'm going to have Lacey place a rubber dental dam because I don't want any of the amalgam filling pieces rinsing down your throat as I remove it. There's this small metal piece that fits against your gums, surrounding the molar." He shows it to me. "Then we'll connect the frame to that, with this rubber piece stretched over it and expose only that molar. This should take 30 minutes or less, no big deal, and the newer composite filling will be stronger and look nicer too." Lacey starts jamming the metal piece into my gums and I wince, tensing.

"Ow! Hurts!"

"You can't feel anything, you've been numbed," Lacey frowns.

"No. Hurts. A lot." Deacon peers down at me, poking at my gums gently with one gloved finger.

"Your gums are a little swollen here, possibly affected by the cut from that ring. When we're done I'll give you a prescription for some antibiotics, just in case. We don't want an infection in there. If this is hurting, we'll need to give you another shot. Did you know that studies have shown redheads are more resistant to the effects of local anesthesia? It tends to take more numbing drugs for them, and they usually need up to 20% more anesthesia when being sedated. I should have thought of that. I'm sorry. I was distracted." He sticks me again, working as he talks. "We'll wait a few minutes for this one to kick in."

Finally numb, Lacey places the metal piece on. It doesn't feel like she's jamming it in there when my tender gums are fully numb. I was probably reading into it too much. With the frame and rubber mat in place it's like some sort of medieval torture device. It's hard to breathe and swallow.

Deacon works carefully, I guess, but I'm blinded by the bright light and can't see into my own mouth regardless. There's the grating sound of the drill and Lacey is expertly controlling the water and suction portion. My hands are clenched into my uniform pants as I try to convince my body to breathe calmly and deeply. I know it's all in my head. There's nothing wrong with my nostrils, I can breathe perfectly fine. My brain, however, is panicking, screaming at me that I'm suffocating inside the rubber dental dam. The instruments have moved ever so slightly and water is spraying into my throat and not being suctioned fast enough. I'm trying desperately to control my racing heart and accelerating respiration while also swallowing awkwardly. I can't breathe. I'm choking on water and I can't breathe. *Keep it together, Fern! This could always get worse! You don't need to add a panic attack to the list of ways you've humiliated yourself in the last 3 days!*

The drilling stops and I look up into Deacon's eyes, praying it's almost over.

"Are you ok?" What does he expect me to do? It's not like I can talk with this giant fucking thing in my mouth! *That's what she said. Stop it, Fern!* I gargle and his mouth tightens.

"Lacey." His voice is cold and hard. "Please adjust the suction so the patient can breathe without choking on water." She does, whispering an apology and I gasp, shaking with relief. I blink back the rush of tears and close my eyes, not wanting to see how he's looking at me. I stay that way until they remove the torture device and all through the testing of my bite until they tell me I'm done.

Deacon's voice comes from the direction of the door as

Lacey lowers the chair and brings me back up to a sitting position. "Let me get that prescription sent over right quick. I'll be back." As soon as the door closes I stand up, grabbing a tissue to wipe my eyes then mouth.

"I apologize," Lacey says. "I don't want you to think that was on purpose. I'd never do that. I didn't realize the suction had moved."

I nod at her. "I know. It's fine. Except for the unintentional drowning, you're good at your job. Thank you." I leave, not waiting for Deacon. I'm not running away, per se, I just have to get away from all the people before I break down. Whether anyone wants to admit it or not, I'm judged more harshly as a woman in uniform. I can't look weak or overly emotional with an audience.

I walk briskly, knowing running will draw more attention, until I'm outside and out of view, then I sink to the ground, letting my head drop between my knees. My lungs are working overtime and my heart feels like it's trying to pump its way out of my chest. I clench my hands into fists, squeezing my fingers together so hard my nails dig into my palms. This is so stupid. At least I'm alone.

And then I'm not.

I'm pretty sure thinking that willed the door open and drew the feet towards me. If only I could use my powers for good! There's a crunch of broken bits of asphalt beneath the shoes and then knees clad in blue scrubs drop to the ground in front of me. I can't look. I can't bear to see who is witnessing my embarrassment, even though I know who it has to be with my shit luck, and I'm working too hard to get my anxiety under control. Warm hands reach for me and I find myself drawn into the most perfect, calming, comforting hug.

38

4

DEACON

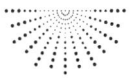

When I came back to an empty room, I immediately ran for the parking lot, hoping to catch Fern before she could drive away. I don't know why I keep trying. It's not like me to put this much effort in with so many signs that I shouldn't. I can't stop thinking about her though. So I run. But she's not driving away. She's collapsed on the ground out of sight of the door. Her whole body is trembling and her breathing is ragged. I pull her into my arms, tucking her face against my neck. It's instinct. Her cheeks are damp with tears. I slow my breathing, running my hand down her back in rhythm with my inhales and exhales. Daisy used to have the same problem and this always helped. I figure, if it worked for my sister's anxiety attacks, it's likely to help Fern too. Slowly her breathing begins to match mine and her fists relax until she's holding me back. She smells bright, like mint and flowers. When she pulls away, I miss the feeling of her in my arms, the sense that I was needed.

"I'm sorry," she whispers.

"For what?" She shakes her head, still not looking at me. "Fern?" I tip her chin up, her skin silky under my fingertips. Her eyes meet mine and she looks down again, this time with the hint of a smile on one side of her lips.

"Don't look at me! It's not fair! You're so damn sexy in your stupid dorky glasses and I can't remember all the reasons why it's better if I stay away."

"Then don't. Forget them. Or at least tell me what they are, over dinner, so I can tell you why your reasons are shit."

"We shouldn't. That's not how this was supposed to go. You don't have anonymous sex with a stranger," she gulps awkwardly, "and then want to go back and cuddle the next night and wake up in his arms and think about him constantly and have dinner dates and live happily ever after!" I have to fight back a smile at the way the impassioned speech was affected by her half-numb mouth.

"Who is making these rules and why do we have to listen to them? I have good rebuttals, I'm sure of it. We need to talk." I brush a loose tendril off of her face, taking a second to appreciate the elegant line of her neck with her hair pulled up. "And I want to hear more about your thing with glasses for sure. I'd be happy to ditch the contacts. But I have to get back to the clinic. Here," I give her my card, "that's my number. Text me. Don't make me look your number up on your paperwork. It's unethical, but I'll do it." She finally gives me a real smile and even lopsided and swollen it's as if the sun has broken over the horizon, brightening everything it touches. I bring my lips to her cheek, prolonging the contact for one more moment before I go back to work.

I don't find it hard to focus on work for the rest of the day. It's not that Fern isn't on my mind, she is, but I've always been able to compartmentalize and take care of the tasks at hand. I'm good at my job and I want to succeed. Being driven and focused is a big part of who I am, no use pretending otherwise. Lacey finds me at the end of the day, right before I'm about to head out.

"Dr. Coleman? I wanted to apologize."

"Yes?" She looks taken aback. I imagine she was expecting me to tell her it's quite alright at the mere mention of an apology, but that's not how I work. One, she hadn't actually apologized yet. And two, simply saying it's fine doesn't fix anything.

"I was rude to your…girlfriend?" It comes out sounding like a question, as if she's seeking confirmation. "That was very unprofessional of me. I'm also sorry about the suction. It wasn't intentional, but I should have been paying closer attention. It won't happen again."

"Personal relationships aside, you recognized the issue and fixed it. That's all I can ask. I'll see you tomorrow."

I could have explained that Fern is not my girlfriend, but that's none of her business. Plus, I don't rightly know what Fern is to me. I don't take my phone out to check my messages until I'm in my car. I do have one from an unfamiliar number, area code 757.

Unknown: This is Fern
Unknown: I can't have dinner—I'm on duty
Unknown: Probably for the best anyway since my mouth is tender and I'm still pretty embarrassed about earlier

Me: What are you embarrassed about? And duty doesn't get you out of dinner, just dinner tonight

I wait for a response, saving her in my contacts, but after 5 minutes I decide to head back to the hotel. No matter what Fern says, I'll still need to go "home," and I need to eat at some point. Traffic going into Waikiki on a Monday evening isn't too bad. It hasn't even been a week and I'm already growing tired of the hotel life. I need to find a place to live. I need to get out a little more so I can decide where I want to live first. By the time I'm changed and walking down Kalakaua in search of dinner, my phone vibrates in my pocket. As a practice in patience and delayed gratification, I make myself wait until I'm seated before I check.

The Shining One: You mean other than nearly having a panic attack during a routine dental procedure and having a meltdown in the parking lot?

Me: Rubber dental dams can make it feel like you're suffocating even when the tech isn't unintentionally drowning you. And no one saw.

The Shining One: You did

Me: Any opportunity to hold you is fine by me.

The Shining One: I didn't say thank you
The Shining One: Thanks for helping me calm down and not making fun of me. That's the second time—how do you know how to do that?

*Me: I would never
make fun of you.
Me: My sister Daisy
used to have panic
attacks a lot. NBD
Me: Tomorrow-does
6 work or should
it be later?*

*The Shining One: Make it
6:30 so I have time to drive
down there*

*Me: I'm picking
you up.*

*The Shining One: This isn't
going to be some big fancy
thing, is it?*

*Me: Wear whatever
you want.
Be comfortable.
No pressure.
Just a regular ol' dinner*

*The Shining One: Ok
The Shining One: I've gotta
get ready to stand watch.
I'll see you tomorrow*

Me: Tomorrow

I spend my quiet, solo dinner thinking about Fern. It's necessary to figure out what I want out of this. I can't give a successful rebuttal to her concerns if I don't know what end result I'm hoping for. What I do know, for certain, is that I don't want Fern to be an anonymous one night stand. I'm not a particularly emotional person, and romance is not my forte, but something in my gut is telling me that more time with Fern will be good. I know there are a lot of things that are trying to stack up in the "con" column but I'm not going to ignore the strength of our immediate, powerful attraction. It wasn't simply that I thought Fern was beautiful. There was something about her that drew me in ,and it's still happening.

I work through my arguments and feelings through dinner, back in the hotel room, on my morning drive, and during breaks at the clinic. I go back to my room to change and get ready for the date and then drive back to Pearl Harbor to pick her up. She dropped me a pin so I'd know where the USS Decatur is. I definitely don't know my way around base yet. I park, thinking I might go across the brow and meet her on the ship but she is already in the parking lot. And she's not alone.

He's taller than I am, short blond hair, more lean than muscular, in uniform. Their body language reminds me of this Sandra Bullock movie Daisy made me watch with her every time she went through a break-up. The guy is definitely "leaning." Jealousy flares up, like a bed of hot coals in my stomach. I have no right to feel possessive, I know that. The feeling is there though. Fern is wearing shorts, a loose tank top and sneakers. I love her legs. They're long and shapely, perfectly displayed in the short denim. Her bright auburn hair is pulled up in a ponytail that falls down her back. Somehow she is just as gorgeous in casual clothes as she was in that little black dress. She sees me and waves, but it seems hesitant. I wish I knew if it's because of me or the other guy. She's still talking to him as I approach.

"Ok, well my date is here. It was nice seeing you again. Maybe I'll see you around."

"You can count on it." He glances at me and steps so he's blocking me, physically, from the conversation. "See ya, Snaggletooth Tiger."

The moment he's walking away I pull her against me, claiming her lips. She's with me tonight, not that asshole. There's no resistance, Fern presses her body into me. She tastes like toothpaste and the way she responds to my kiss makes my competitive side feel like I've won.

"Hi," she sighs when I pull away.

"I've been thinking about doing that since I woke up to an empty bed on Sunday." She pinches the plump flesh of her bottom lip between her teeth, guilt coloring her eyes. I let her feel guilty. Maybe now she won't ghost me again. I take her hand and walk us back to my car.

"So that was your ex, huh? The Snaggletooth guy you told me about? Why exactly does he call you something unkind and unflattering while trying to get you to see him again?" I open her door for her, waiting to shut it until she's sitting.

"He doesn't mean it that way. It's just, you know, my overlapping teeth and orange hair." She gestures towards herself flippantly. I frown.

"Except it's critical and unnecessary. You have a great smile and your hair is not orange. If he likes you, why wouldn't he make it a point to tell you the things about you that he's into instead of making you the butt of an inside joke?" She squirms in her seat, knotting her fingers together. I navigate us out of the parking lot and head off base. "He could have called you Freyja, the Norse goddess of love and beauty. She was also called The Shining One and is a redhead that's been worshipped throughout history for her beauty and wisdom. He could have come up with something that would always remind you of something intimate, between the two of you." I reach across and gently pull her hands apart, weaving our fingers together. She squeezes lightly, angling her body towards me.

"Hell, he could outright compliment you, foregoing the juvenile nicknames completely. Instead he chose to belittle you. If it were me, I might point out that your eyes are the color of the Irish moss that grows in Louisville. I could point

45

out any number of things I like about your body. It would be hard to choose only one, Fern." She dips her head slightly, a light pink flush blooming on her cheeks. "Maybe I'd admit that I find you effortlessly sexy, and I've replayed Saturday night a thousand times in my head. But that's just me. I was never the guy who pulled a girl's pigtails to get her to notice me. My Mamaw always told me a spoonful of honey was more effective than a gallon of vinegar."

"You're certainly generous with the honey." I sneak a glance at her while stopped at a red light. She's no longer tense and there's a soft smile on her lips. Mamaw is always right. I pull into Nico's Pier 38, leaving the car running.

"Wait here. I called an order in, I'll run in and pick it up." I jog in and back out, not wanting to waste any of our time together. I place the food in the backseat next to the bag the concierge helped me put together. I like planning, but I'm not particularly romantic and had no idea where to start. That guy is good. I park at the hotel and Fern looks like she's debating whether or not to say something.

"Are we…" she looks around the parking garage.

I jump in, laughing, once I realize what she's worried about. "Dinner wasn't code for sex. But I already pay for the hotel parking so I thought we could walk from here."

She giggles. "The thought of going up to your room wasn't terrible! I was just confused since you asked me to dinner."

"Dinner is the plan, promise. I'm a straightforward kind of guy." I grab the bags and Fern slips her small hand into mine. It feels right. I like strolling side by side, hand in hand. I find us a spot on the beach and spread out the blanket. Fern kicks off her shoes and sits. She's as pretty as a postcard perched on the edge of the blanket with the ocean behind her. I sneak a photo of her and then chide myself for it. Why did I do that? I don't keep mementos of girls I date. Whatever. I'm not here to analyze myself. I shake it off and I hand her a chilled bottle of Shaka Tea and a box of food. "If you don't like fish, this dinner is going to be a bust. I should have asked you, but I wanted to have everything taken care of. It came highly recommended." I feel a seed of worry take root. I'd hate for my desire to control all the variables to be the reason the date is unsuccessful. She pops a piece of the furikaki crusted, pan-seared ahi tuna into her mouth, the tip of her pink tongue darting out to catch an errant sesame seed.

Her groan of pleasure goes straight to my dick. He needs to keep it together. "It's delicious!"

We sit, watching the waves while we eat. The sun, sinking lower towards the horizon, bathes Fern in a golden glow. She takes our empty food containers over to a trash can and when she comes back she makes herself comfortable between my outstretched legs, leaning back into me. It feels good. She's constantly surprising me.

"Let's hear those rebuttals, Dr. Coleman."

"I can't really give rebuttals until you give your objections. Shouldn't you tell me why you think this isn't worth pursuing?"

"Right." She sighs. "I can do that. Well, for one, we live in two different places. This is essentially doomed before it even starts. Two, I never date guys in the military. Anymore. So that's no good." She's ticking the points off on her long fingers. Have I ever thought someone's hands were pretty before? Hers are.

"You don't really know me. And this is going to sound like a line, like I want validation but it's not," she assures me. She tenses as if preparing for the worst. "I need to be totally up front with you. I can honestly say, and not out of self-pity, that no one has ever gotten close to me and wanted to stick around. I repel people. I'm self-centered and weird and prone to embarrassing myself, as you've already seen. This was really good for what it was. Like, *really* good. I'm more than satisfied to say you're my one and only one night stand. Why ruin it by changing the expectations?" Her shoulders are tight and she's clenching her fingers tight enough that her knuckles are white.

As she finishes talking, her voice sounds lighthearted while her body language is expressing the exact opposite. If she was truly ready to walk away, she wouldn't care about what I think. I brush the end of her ponytail away from her neck and place a line of light kisses down towards her shoulder, my fingers tracing her collarbone. I'm not going to make this easy for her. I don't mind playing a little dirty.

"I'm not sure why it matters that we live in two different cities. You're here now. At least for the duration of RIMPAC. Why should we put so much emphasis on the future that we kill the present? Especially when we know being in the Navy means we'll both be somewhere else before too long." I move to the other side of her neck, kissing my way down to her other shoulder. I keep talking, my lips so close to her skin that every breath is full of her mint and floral scent. "Clearly Snaggletooth Guy is in the military. Why does that asshat get a pass but I don't?" I move back up her neck, my lips gliding along her jaw as her head falls back onto my shoulder. I kiss her softly, her lips cool and her fingertips warm when she slides them up along my face. God, I love how she touches me. I press my mouth firmly to hers before speaking into her. "You could never repel me, Fern. This *is* really good. I don't want to let other people's labels dictate what I can and cannot do."

"Now you're speaking my language," she whispers, smiling against me. "Can we go back to your room?"

FERN

Deacon packs up our beach picnic but he keeps finding ways to touch me and kiss me. It's a short walk back to the hotel, but it feels too long. Every time he looks at me, I burn a little more. I can't help myself. His touch sends little paths of fire along my skin and his words are seared right on my heart. I'm warning myself to be careful, to hold back, to keep some emotional distance, but I've never been good at that. He still doesn't know me very well. He speaks a good game but this could still be all about the physical. Clearly seeing me with John caused some jealousy. Deacon could merely be a competitive guy who doesn't like to be beaten. It shouldn't, but it makes me feel good that he's jealous. I've never had someone like me that much. I can't lose my head and I need to get a super glue tight grip on my heart. That doesn't change how much I want him. Simply walking next to him is doing things to me.

We step into the elevator, thankfully alone, and he presses me into the wall, kissing me hungrily. I slide my hands up into his t-shirt, dragging it up his delicious torso until I can pull it over his head. It is not fair how good he looks.

"You can't undress me in the elevator, Fern." The curve of his lips is downright naughty.

"Who says? Maybe you just came back from the beach. I don't know if you've noticed, but Honolulu is very casual. No one who sees you shirtless is going to complain, trust me. If anything, they'll probably thank me. You could say I'm doing a public service." I pull him down to kiss me again and his arms wrap around my back, arching it and pulling me tight against the hard rod in his shorts. I back out of the open elevator door, dragging him with me as he tries to stay connected to my lips. I giggle, then Deacon trips, making me laugh even harder. "We'd probably already be in your room if we were walking like normal people."

"This is more fun." He lifts me up, carrying me and the bag easily. I wrap my legs around him, holding on for dear life while he jogs to the door. Once inside he drops the bag and pushes my back into the wall, his kisses no longer playful. I nip at his bottom lip, capturing it with my teeth, and he groans as he slides the band from my hair. His fingers massage my scalp, running through my wind tangled locks, tugging lightly, while his tongue explores my mouth. God, everything he does to me feels too good. He duplicates my actions from the elevator, sliding his large hands up my torso and tossing my tank top away.

"Shit, Fern. You weren't wearing a bra all night?"

"I told you. My boobs are so small…" he interrupts me, talking between peppering kisses across my chest.

"I would really prefer it if you would stop disparaging the girls." He catches my nipple with his teeth, making me gasp with pleasure. "They're perfect just as they are and you're going to give them a complex. I have to pay them extra attention, to be sure they haven't been hurt by your callousness." Tongue and teeth graze my skin until I'm burning, desperate for more. I try to wriggle out of his grasp, to reach the floor, to move us, but he's holding me firmly in his strong arms.

"Deacon. Please?"

"Is this not enough, Shining One?"

"I want more. I need to see all of you. And the thermostat is digging into my back." He doesn't put me down but walks us over to the bed, lowering me gently to the mattress. Deacon makes quick work of the rest of our clothes. "Gosh, you're sexy," I blurt out as I put my arms behind my head and drink in the sight of his naked form. "You can't look like that naked and not know that, right?" He grins, eyes crinkling at the corners, and without the beard he has these hollows under his high cheekbones. *DAMN.*

"Do you like what you see, Fern?"

"I'd like it more if you'd bring it down here," I grumble.

"So this is how you want it this time? Playful? I'll tell you a little secret," he pounces on me, rolling us over so I'm stretched out on top of him, "I'm a sucker for sex and laughter." He runs his fingers down my sides, poking until he finds a tickle spot and then exploiting it until I'm squealing. I'm squirming and bucking, trying to wiggle away from his advances and then I'm sliding over his impressive erection. We both freeze. I suck in a shaky breath, eyes wide, and then do it again. "You're playing with fire, Fern." His voice is low and gravelly, vibrating in his chest.

"Am I? I thought it was your dick." I rub against him once more and bring my mouth to his chest, licking and kissing until he's the one writhing. Making Deacon lose himself is my new favorite thing. It makes me feel powerful. I climb off him, standing by the bed to rifle through the bedside drawer in search of a condom. He lies still, watching, that beautiful member standing at attention for me. Rolling the condom down, I'm relishing my control, and then it's inexplicably gone. Faster than I'm prepared for, Deacon is off the bed. I'm bent over, pressed into the mattress edge, and he's pushing my legs open with his knee. The rough tug on my hair as he wraps it around his hand coincides with him sliding himself between my legs. My body tingles in anticipation but he teases me, gliding back and forth, spreading my arousal. It's maddening. I'm a pulsing ball of need and his dominance just turns me on more. He pulls firmly on my hair and gently bites my neck, teeth digging into my tendon as he finally pushes into me. A moan escapes me, unbidden. He pulls me back against him, back to torso, releasing my hair so he can slide his arm around me. He's kneading my breast, punctuating every slow, deep thrust with a pinch of my nipple. I feel like an instrument under his capable hands and he is a fucking prodigy.

The need for his touch is aching in me when he finally slides his hand lower. I gasp as he adds tiny zigzags over my clitoris. I'm overwhelmed by the sensations. He's hitting a spot, deep inside me, that I didn't know craved his touch. Fingers nudge me closer to the brink and he holds our bodies close, his movements languid and sensual. I can't touch him so I settle for bracing my hands against the mattress and pushing back into him. Thankfully he doesn't keep up a steady stream of chatter. Dirty talk is fine, I guess, but I don't want anything distracting me from the way he's making me feel. Heat is building low in my body and a wave of liquid heat is cresting inside of me.

"More. That's so good, just…more." I can't manage anything else. I'm so close. Deacon has kept the pace the same but he's thrusting harder and deeper. It's all almost too much when he rubs harder on my clit. Almost. He hits me just right and it's as if my body shatters into a million pinpricks of light. I can't do anything but moan, my muscles tightening and spasming uncontrollably. Deacon holds me tight, arching into me. I can feel his release even as I'm floating down from my own.

When he finishes I expect him to pull out, take care of the condom, and stroll back in, cocky and pleased with himself. Instead, he turns me in his arms, all strength and gracefulness, resting me gently on the bed and lowering himself down on top of me. There are more points of contact than not. I feel almost giddy. His lips are soft and his tongue slides a lazy path around mine. It's affection and comfort, satiety but still desire.

"I'm not crushing you, am I?"

"Crush away. I like it." He kisses my cheeks, my chin, and the tip of my nose.

"Be right back." Without his weight pressing me down I move up on the bed, my skin sliding against the cool sheets until my head is resting on a pillow. When he comes back, Deacon lies next to me, pressing a soft kiss to my forehead. I turn onto my side and run my fingers through his hair.

"It's shorter." I comment. His hair is thick and soft.

"I was on leave. It got a bit unruly. It was nice to not think about my haircut or shaving for a little bit. I had to get it cut on Sunday, before I started work."

"I thought you were *safe* because your look didn't say military."

"What about…" he starts but I interrupt him, knowing exactly what he's going to ask.

"John is in the Navy too. Our break up is the reason I avoid military guys." I'm still running my fingers through his hair. I have this crazy thought that I wish I could be even closer, an almost need to be more physically connected to him.

"I guess it's a good thing I put off that haircut." His smile is so damn cute, I can't help but return it. It has a hint of mischief to it I can't resist. I bet Deacon was a naughty little boy, and that smile kept him from getting into too much trouble. "What happened that made you anti-military?" He closes his eyes, letting his head fall back while I tickle his scalp.

"We worked together. When he got his orders, I thought it was great that he got San Diego because I was leaning towards the West Coast for my next set of orders. But then he broke up with me. He said what we had wasn't worth the effort to maintain long distance. Really I think he wanted to be free to hook up after moving and during deployment port calls." As I talk his fingers skate across my skin, caressing lightly. I like the roughness of his hands, like the soft scratch of his beard the first time.

"He didn't want to be tied down. You really have to be committed to maintain a relationship during deployments.

That's not John. Balancing the demands of two careers and battling two sets of orders is a lot to deal with. The biggest problem with dating a guy in the military was that John dumped me before he left the ship, so his remaining time, up until he detached, made for a really uncomfortable Ward Room. I don't want to go through that again."

"I'm *not* a SWO. For now I'm attached to a shore dental clinic. Later I'll likely deploy with a carrier. Would we end up in the same place then?" I can't keep my hands off of him, running my fingers through his hair and over the contours of his face, wrapping my arms over his shoulders and caressing the muscles of his back.

"No, I like working on the small boys. Platform is important to me; I stick to Destroyers and Cruisers. Carriers can have 6,000 people on board! I like the intimacy of a smaller Ward Room. I know who I'm working with and recognize the majority of the crew on sight."

"So what I'm hearing is we won't be working together, and we have very different jobs."

"True."

"Sounds to me like that issue has been resolved." He traces his fingers along the tattoo on my ribcage. "What's the significance here? This is a fern, of course. But what about the flowers? Do they represent something?"

"Nope." I laugh. "It's embarrassing but there is no significance at all. It means nothing. I knew these girls in middle school. We were pretty close, or at least I thought we were. I considered them my best friends, until they told me I was a stuck up bitch and stopped talking to me. It was pretty devastating. I was alone and never really recovered. I made it through high school without any close relationships." He presses his lips to my jaw. Yeesh, he's sweet!

"Fast forward to our senior year and we're all in the same English class. They were talking during class about getting tattoos together. They looked me up and down, very dismissive with a heaping dose of derision, and said they wouldn't waste their time inviting me since I'd never get a tattoo. It pissed me off. A lot." He rests his hand on my ribs, grounding me with its weight and warmth. "I told them to book me an appointment with theirs because I was in. Made it out to be for old times sake, and not because I'm screwed up. So, that's me in a nutshell. I dislike being told what to do or who I am so much that I got this incredibly painful floral tattoo on my ribcage to convince two girls who hated me they were wrong about me. You picked a winner, Deacon. Don't say I didn't warn you." He laughs, that sexy, genuine sound that settles in my chest and feels like it's blooming.

"They suck! But I think you're hilarious and oddly bad ass. You subvert expectations. I like that about you."

No one has *ever* liked that about me. I slide my palm over his cheek. "I kind of miss the scruff. But losing the stubble in exchange for the glasses is more than fair."

"The glasses really do it for you, huh?"

"It's not like I have a thing for glasses! Or at least, I didn't think I did. I'm not ticking off boxes here. But you in glasses?" I fan myself theatrically. "It is stupid hot! It makes me want to force you to wear contacts everywhere so no one else can see you like that!" *Shit.* Classic Fern, the master of too much too soon. I feel my eyes widen, eyebrows raising on their own, and I nibble my lip nervously.

"That right there," he brings his face closer and kisses me, teasing my lip out of the grip of my teeth. "I dig it. I don't mind the possessive jokes. I like them! You make me feel very possessive, Fern. I don't want anyone else touching you. I want to be the only one kissing these lips." He's giving me goosebumps with the way he's kissing me. "I love your lips."

"But RIMPAC," I argue, half-heartedly, surrendering to another kiss. He is too good at this and I'm losing focus.

"RIMPAC is 6 weeks, right? Do you think this is worth that?" He's studying me and I go with what I want, not what I think is best. I nod in agreement. "So, we get to know each other and explore the island together, whenever you're free

Now that I'm not stressing myself out, worrying about what we are and where it's going and how I can screw things up, Deacon is easy to talk to. Often, when I'm talking to someone I don't know very well, I get so nervous about talking too much or going too deep or making things weird that I forget to keep the conversation moving. I space on asking questions and babble on nervously, unintentionally making everything about me. Deacon sets me at ease, though, and I find myself asking questions because I want to know as much about him as possible. I forget to be nervous because I'm so interested in what he's saying.

We touch on our families and what it was like where we grew up. We both sang in the choir in high school, most comfortable in the group setting, and we nerd out over our favorite musical theater songs. We both play guitar and were far from popular. I still didn't believe someone that looks like Deacon could be a late bloomer but he digs up an old photo his mom sent him. He was so endearingly awkward! He gained the height all at once but hadn't filled out. He was skinny and stoop shouldered with floppy hair and glasses. I don't understand how girls didn't see all of his attractive qualities though. They're still there if you look closely. Then I had to show him my high school photo, sharing the misery. I don't think I look much different now except I am less gangly. I also grew all at once and had a period where I felt like I was mostly elbows and knees. He runs his finger over my screen, taking in my dumb haircut and questionable fashion choices.

"I still wouldn't have seen anyone else when you walked in a room. But I wouldn't have been confident enough to talk to you."

"Are we looking at the same picture? Everything about me is tragic. I think you look sweet though. I would have had a crush on you. And I probably would have thought I actually had a chance with teenage Deacon!"

"I think it's pretty clear you have better than a chance with adult Deacon." He laughs, pressing a light kiss to my shoulder.

"I'm still not sure why, if I'm being totally honest. If I had seen you first, I wouldn't have given you a second glance." His face falls and I rush to explain. "Not because you're not incredibly good looking, but because of it! One look at you would have told me that there was no way in hell you'd talk to me so I would have immediately moved on. If I was looking, which I'm typically not, it would have been for someone more like me." Deacon stands up and takes my hand, leading me back inside to the bed. He pulls me against his chest and falls back onto the bed, taking me with him. Lying in a heap, he brushes my hair away from my face and presses his lips to mine, eyes searching.

"I want you to tell me what you meant by all of that. Why wouldn't I talk to you? And who is someone more like you?" I squirm, his words making me uncomfortable, but he continues to hold me gently, tracing his fingertips across my face.

"Clearly you're out of my league, Deacon. I mean, look at you! Your face, that body." I exhale in a huff. "I can't compare! And typically guys that are as hot as you are would never even look at me. They want showy: obvious sex appeal and the confidence that goes with knowing everyone wants you. I'd go for someone more like me. Someone...normal. That's me. Normal. Very average. My hair is too red. My skin is super pale. I'm not very curvy. I suck in social situations. I make everything weird. I don't have any close friends—" He stops me with a kiss. It's more than a kiss. It's like he's refuting my words with his touch. His fingers run through my hair, dance across my skin, skim down my sides and then he wraps me in his arms. When he finally separates our lips, ending a panty-melting kiss, his eyes look stern.

"We may only have the next six weeks together, but during that time, I want you to promise me that this stops. I don't want to hear any more about why you're not enough or somehow undeserving. When those thoughts come up, you need to replace them with what *I* think. Can you do that?"

"What *you* think?"

"Yes. It seems like I know a little better than you do what I have in my arms. So you listen hard, Fern McClellan. Your hair is like that burning glow at sunset. Women pay a lot of money to fake having hair like yours." He runs his fingers through my hair, pulling lightly so my scalp tingles.

"Your skin is perfect." His rough hands give me goosebumps, running over my skin as he talks. "I dreamt about how it looks against these sheets, how it feels under my hands, how it tastes." The light touch of his tongue on my neck makes me shiver.

"I love how your body looks, exactly the way it is." He caresses each part he mentions, setting me ablaze with desire. "Those long legs, the swell of your hips, the curve of your ass, the way your tits fit in my hands, every bit of your sexy, delicate little body turns me on. And I know you won't believe me ,but it's not just me. I wasn't the only guy watching you at that bar. I had to bribe the bartender to put me up on the stage next to you because I couldn't get up the nerve to talk to you on my own and I couldn't bear to let one of them get to you first. I like your quirks. I want to be with you in social situations. I. Like. You." He emphasizes each word with a kiss and I melt into him.

I don't know what to do with all of his words. They're too much. Too kind. Too flattering. For now I store them, soaking up the way he sees me. What would it be like if I saw myself that way too?

6

DEACON

I like waking up with Fern in my arms. She fits so nicely. I like the contrast of my tan arms against her ivory abdomen. I like it even more because she wasn't prepared to stay and we ended up sleeping sans clothes again. It's no hardship. It probably feeds my ego too. Seeing this beautiful woman next to me validates that I'm no longer that awkward, shy kid. If teenage Deacon could see me now he'd probably cream himself. She snuggles in closer, murmuring in her sleep. I probably shouldn't have asked her to stay. I keep pushing things a little more than what I usually allow. It's a bit much for a second date and likely confuses things more when it comes to our relationship. Still, I needed a do-over. Waking up, expecting to be holding Fern like this, only to find an empty spot next to me with no explanation, bothered me more than I want to admit. I had to replace that image in my head. *This* doesn't have to happen again. I'm sure we can slip into normal dating routines. Right?

I wish it wasn't necessary, but we have to leave this bed and get ready for work. Fern is very affectionate in the morning and it makes it that much harder to be motivated to begin this regular, mundane Tuesday. She's soft and warm, pressed close to me. She keeps running her hands all over my body, kissing me sleepily. She rolls over stretching slowly. When she scoots back, her ass finding my morning wood, her eyes get this dangerous glint, watching me over her shoulder. I'm caressing her silky skin, telling myself to get up, and then Fern is sliding between my legs and taking me in her mouth. Those lips. That tongue. She's teasing and playful, getting me going, then she's not. Fuck me, she's not messing around. The things she is doing to me are overloading my senses. I groan, my muscles clenching as she works me over.

"Fuck, Fern, I…" I have no idea what I was going to say. There are no words. I look down the length of my body and her silvery green eyes meet mine. She moans into me, taking me deeper and I'm primed to explode. The way she's watching me is so fucking sexy and my head falls back as I let go, groaning out her name. She slides up my body, blanketing me with her own and kissing me deeply.

"Good morning." Her eyes are bright and I love how happy she is to have wrecked me first thing in the morning. I wish I was inside of her right now. Actually…

"Deacon, what are you…" she starts as I flip her onto her back, bringing my tongue to her wet center.

"You taste so fucking delicious." Getting me off clearly turned her on and I lap it up, making her fist her hands into my hair. Having her at my mercy now tops my list of favorite things. It doesn't take long until she's crying out, her body shaking underneath me. I wouldn't mind starting every day with the taste of Fern on my tongue. Her hair is wild, her body is relaxed and her expression is blissful. I wish I could freeze time.

Dressed and holding hands, we grab a quick breakfast downstairs before taking extra coffee to go. I drop Fern off at the pier since she needs time to get into uniform in her state room. It feels very couple-y, as Fern would say, standing outside the car, kissing her before we go our separate ways for work. I'm surprised by how much I like it. Her two friends pass us, also in civilian clothes and interrupt our kiss, catcalling.

"Foxy Dentist!" The brunette calls.

"You know his name is Deacon, Brooklyn. Be nice." The blonde frowns.

"Sure, but if the name fits..." She winks at me. "Come on, Fernie! Time to start our day."

Fern gives me one last, lingering kiss and follows after them, looking back over her shoulder before climbing the stairs to the brow. How'd she know I'd still be watching? I shoot her a quick text, before she goes down inside the ship.

Me: Can I see you tonight?

The Shining One: You saw me 5 seconds ago

Me: And? I already want to see you again. So...tonight?

The Shining One: Ok, but I'm picking you up this time
The Shining One: I'll be outside your hotel at 5:30. Wear jeans and closed toed shoes. Boots if you have them.

Me: Should I be worried?

The Shining One: This time, I've got you

Waiting outside the hotel, the anticipation that's been building all day starts to take a turn into nerves. I don't like to be at someone else's mercy. I'm always the one in control. I shove my hands into my pockets to keep from fidgeting while I scan the incoming cars. Someone on a motorcycle waves me over. I hope they're not going to ask for directions, I won't be any help. The black helmet comes off and it's Fern beckoning me. Did I know a sexy redhead on a motorcycle was a thing for me? It *definitely* is now.

She's in black leather, her hair braided down her back, and I can add this to the array of "times when Fern turns me on" mental pictures I'm storing up. She puts the kickstand down and climbs off. It's a real-deal motorcycle, not a street bike or little scooter. Seeing her confidently in control of such a big machine is an even bigger turn on. I may have problems. I've never been so constantly horny.

"Here," she removes a mesh bag clipped to the extra seat on the back and hands me a helmet. I take it from her and she digs in the saddlebags, bringing out something leather. The scent carried to me by the breeze says it's real leather and it feels buttery in my hands when she gives it to me.

"Where did this come from?" I balance the helmet on the seat so I can pull the jacket on. The fit is perfect.

"I *knew* that would look good on you!" I'll take the compliment, but she didn't answer my question.

"Fern?" I tilt my head and her cheeks flush. She's definitely avoiding answering me on purpose.

"I didn't want you riding without one. This is safer."

"Can you rent gear?"

"Some places," she hedges. "I was going to rent you a helmet, but the guy who rented me his bike said he'd buy the helmet from me when I'm done. He'll get an extra he can add to his listing, and I break even. Win win." She looks nervous, waiting for my reaction.

"So you bought a helmet for me to use *and* a leather jacket?" There's that pretty pink flush again. I press my lips to hers briefly. No touch is ever enough. Should I be concerned about the intensity of this craving for her? Can it ever be satisfied? "This is definitely too much, but thank you. I've never had a leather jacket before."

"It's too bad you live in Hawai'i so you won't get many opportunities to wear it. It suits you. With the glasses you have this whole bad boy slash nerdy professor thing going on. You're basically my tailor made fantasy right now." She steps closer, adjusting the lapels on my jacket.

I grin at that. I like the idea of being Fern's fantasy. "I take it you didn't find a place to rent what you have on?"

"Oh, no. This is all mine. I brought it with me."

"Do you own a motorcycle?" That is even hotter than her renting one while here.

"I do! I have a Harley Softail Slim. She's gold and my most prized possession."

"You're a legitimate bad ass! There you go, subverting expectations again. I like it. Take me for a ride, Fern." She bites her lip suggestively and the fact that her mind went there gets me even more — maybe because mine did too. Dirty minds think alike. I am really, really into this girl. Fern is full of surprises and the more I know about her the deeper I want to dig.

We climb on the Harley and Fern directs us through downtown and farther east. The flashes of ocean to our right are a calm turquoise. We curve around what has to be the southern tip of O'ahu, if my mental map is correct and the color of the water is slowly changing. The cliffs are smooth, stratified ledges jutting out into the ocean on a completely undeveloped portion of the coastline. It's peaceful, if not a little strange after leaving heavily populated Honolulu. The roar of the motor, holding onto Fern as she expertly navigates the curves of the highway, and the unparalleled vistas before us are all unexpectedly awesome. The turquoise of the waves has deepened with crashing, white capped waves. The road climbs and before it turns to head up the coastline, Fern pulls off into the Makapu'u Overlook parking lot. Helmets in hand we stand at the rock wall topped with a metal railing. The ocean is unreal, a deep cobalt blue that shifts to teal and then lighter turquoise as you look up the coast.

"This makes me wish I could paint. It's like being out on the open ocean." Fern shoves her gloves in a pocket and slips her free hand into mine. "It's overwhelming, being surrounded by that much water, nothing else in sight. And at night? The stars are unbelievable. I wish I had a way to adequately capture and express that feeling. The world is so big and I'm so small. Not in a fearful way, but I'm overcome and grateful to be a tiny part of it." Her expression is wistful and so lovely.

"Here," a man speaks next to us, waving his hand towards himself. "Give me your phone, I'll get a picture!" Fern gives him hers and I put my arm around her, tucking her into my side. I like the thought of having a photo of this moment. I silence the voice that wants to ask why. I don't need to question everything or have all the answers.

We stand for a while longer, the only sound the waves crashing at the base of the cliffs. Hunger takes us back to the bike and out onto the open road. This stretch of coast, from Makap'u Point up through Waimānalo is my favorite so far with the towering mountains to our left and the gorgeous ocean to our right. Fern was right. It does make you feel small, but grateful. She takes us into Kailua and parks at a cute little green bungalow in the heart of the busy town. Fern made us a reservation for dinner at Kalapawai Cafe & Deli.

It feels good to set the helmets aside and strip off the leather jacket. Fern has on a little tank top underneath and it's hard not to reach across the table to touch all that bared skin. The waitress comes to get our drink orders and Fern asks for water so I do the same but she can sense the question I haven't asked.

She lifts one shoulder in a shrug. "I don't drink much. I don't really like beer and I know absolutely nothing about wine. I figured water was safest, especially since I'm driving. You don't have to do without because of me."

"Nah, I'm not much of a drinker either. And I don't know

about you, but ever since I got here I feel like I can't get enough water! I'm drinking all day long, but I always feel thirsty!"

"Me too! I thought everyone carrying around reusable water bottles was an eco thing but now I get how necessary it is! My friend, Norah, said eventually your body will get used to the heat and humidity here. Coincidentally, she also recommended this place. She said everything is delicious, but I'm going to get the curried shepherd's pie because that's her favorite. She hasn't let me down yet!"

Dinner is delicious and relaxed. We have similar stories about ridiculous, unintentionally hilarious family road trips. I laugh loudly, scaring the older couple at the table behind us when she tells me how things would inevitably go very wrong and her dad's catchphrase was to angrily yell, "We're making memories!" Our dads sound very similar and she has me rolling, describing her family dynamics. They sound like they'd be a lot of fun to be around and it makes me wonder how Fern fits into the mix. She's sunny and fun, but the longer I'm with her the more I see that she puts on a happy face for the sake of those around her. I'm beginning to wonder if it's also to keep them at a distance.

"I'm curious about something but I don't want to upset you. I'm going to ask, but please take it in the kindest, gentlest way possible and know that it's because I want to know you better." I reach for her hand, interlocking our fingers. "It sounds like your family is all pretty funny and upbeat. With parents and siblings like that, why do you seem like you're putting on a happy face to appear that way? What about your growing up in that environment made you this accomplished woman who finds fault in herself?"

I can see as well as hear her sharp intake of breath. "Um," her fingers tighten around mine and I can feel her leg jiggling faintly under the table.

"No judgement. I just wondered."

"It's not the question itself as much as it is that no one, not even my family, has ever seen that before. No one has ever looked at me that closely. I don't know what to do with that. I'm used to being invisible. You're right, my family is light and fun, very jokey and high energy. They're great. Truly. From early childhood, though, I knew that I was different. I didn't really fit. Once I got up in middle school and was faced with hormones, more complicated friendships, and a bigger school, I really started to see that my emotions, my *otherness*, my hurts and worries, were too much." She strokes the back of my hand with her free hand, tracing knuckles with her fingertips.

"My parents couldn't deal with it. I didn't want to burden them, or be seen as the problem kid, so I kept it all to myself. Things were easier when I pretended to be like all of them. I felt like, if I was too much for people that already loved me, there was no hope for anyone else. I figured all my future could hold was being alone." She keeps her eyes down, looking at our hands. "High school was a nightmare. I didn't have anyone I could talk to about it so I kept a lot of depressing, dramatic, angst-filled journals. I was very emo." She laughs sharply and that bitter self-judgment feels like too much acid in my stomach.

"When I left for college I was able to go to the doctor, on my own, without worrying my parents. I, uh," she delays, taking a deep breath, "was diagnosed with pretty severe major depressive disorder. It wasn't connected to any one thing, but it had been going on for so long I genuinely forgot what it felt like to actually be happy. Maybe growing up in the happiest family around while feeling unreasonably sad all the time contributed to that. It made me feel more isolated and broken. Getting on a daily prescription helped immensely. I wish I had talked to someone sooner. Maybe adolescence would have been a little kinder on me if I had been honest about how I was feeling." Her eyes dart up, looking at me and then back to our hands before I can react. I want to go back in time and hug teenage Fern, convince her it will all be okay.

"Even so, it's a part of who I am now. Most people, when

they get to know me with any real depth, pull away and eventually cut off all contact. I guess I'm an acquired taste. I wasn't wrong in thinking I was too much to deal with. I am. It's who I am. Now I keep that happy public persona and people are comfortable around me, as long as they don't get too close. They're good, and I at least can take comfort in the deeper knowledge of who I am and what I've grown from. Even if other people don't like it, there's power in understanding what makes you tick. Just because I'm not for everybody doesn't mean I'm not for somebody. I'm more of a small-number-of-close-people girl than a big-group-of-casual-friends person." She finally meets my eyes, smiling cautiously. It's heartening knowing that she's okay now with who she is and what she needs in relationships. I feel like I know her better. Now I need her to see that.

I slip cash into the bill folder that holds our receipt and stand up, pulling Fern into a hug. Everything she said has me feeling too much. I'm sad for young Fern and I'm proud of Fern now. I need her to know that she's not too much but I don't know how and, regardless, I can't do it here, in the middle of a restaurant.

"Let's get out of here. Come back with me? Or is that too much? I'm probably being ridiculous, I know this isn't how regular dating works but, can we go back to my room?" I bring my lips to hers, the touch soft and far too brief for my liking.

"I did pack some things, in case you invited me back. I thought, we only have six weeks together, might as well make the most of it."

"Good, that's settled. Take us home." I can feel the heat rising on my cheeks as I realize what I said, but Fern is gathering up her gear and doesn't seem to notice. What an idiot! I need to keep a tighter rein on myself, it's dangerous to be careless with words around someone that reads into everything.

The sun is already behind the imposing Ko'olau

Mountains as we make our way up the H-3, but when we exit the tunnel through the mountains, it's blazing orange and pink over the west side. I enjoy seeing Hawai'i like this. Maybe some guys would find it emasculating to ride on a motorcycle behind a woman, but my manhood is secure. Relinquishing my control and letting Fern take care of this date turned out great. Plus, it's nice sitting close, my arms wrapped around her. By the time we're hanging up the motorcycle gear in my room, the need to touch her is all-consuming. There's a lot I want Fern to feel from me. She's setting her boots out of the way and reaching for the zipper to her mesh and leather riding pants when I can't wait any longer. I reach for her.

"Let me help with that." Not that I had any doubt, but she is as sexy out of the motorcycle gear as she is in it. If she has to have on clothes, a thong and tiny tank top are a-okay with me. I carefully unbraid her hair, running my fingers through her long locks, as she unbuttons my shirt. I discard my jeans and lead her to the bed so I can finally hold her the way I've been wanting to all night. Of course, I want her. I always do. But I'm going to let her take the lead tonight. After how she opened up to me, I don't want her to think I'm only putting in time with her to get to the physical.

Once again I'm struck by how perfectly she fits in my arms. Her head is nestled on my shoulder, forehead against my neck and lips pressed to my collarbone. She tips her chin up until we can look in each other's eyes and her kiss is timid. She responds to the movement of my lips until her tongue is slipping against mine and I have to put in real effort to keep things slow and soft. Fuck, she gets me going. She clutches me tightly. It feels like she's right there with me.

"Thank you for sharing with me tonight." I murmur against her lips, not wanting her to retreat. "You should know, the more I get to know you, the more I want to know." She brushes her lips against mine and I suck her lower lip into my mouth, scraping lightly with my teeth. "You're not too much for me, Fern."

7

FERN

This time with Deacon has been so unexpected and fulfilling. Funny how an "I'll show Brooklyn how wrong she is about me" fling has become regular dates, throughout the day texts, nightly hotel sleepovers and a burgeoning sense of self that I never could have dreamed of. Deacon is so patient with me and attentive. He seems determined to make me see myself the way he sees me. I can't even fight it, because I like the way he sees me. I miss him when we're away doing warfare exercises and look forward to seeing him, leaning against his car, waiting for me at the pier when we pull back in to dock. I'm trying not to focus on the looming end date. I don't want that to steal anything from the present, but it's always there in the back of my head, like the hidden clock, ticking behind some unknown wall in my favorite book as a kid. There's only two weeks left.

We're blazing through RIMPAC, pulling in after our latest exercise when I spy a familiar face in the closest parking lot. It felt like it took forever to dock and switch from ship to shore power knowing that Deacon was waiting for me. Ships have been trickling back in all day and everyone is anxious for liberty to start so we can get off the ship. I feel that way in particular because I only have tonight and tomorrow night and then I have Friday duty. At least it's the last of my weekend duties while in Hawai'i. When everything is finally done, I change into a short and airy dress, wanting to feel pretty after days in my coveralls.

I've barely reached Deacon before he lifts me up and swings me around. I'd worry about flashing strangers my underwear, but all I can think about is the feel of his lips on mine and his strong arms around me. He slides me down his front, keeping me close even as he's setting me back on my feet.

"It's straight up dumb how much I missed you." His voice is low and settles even lower in my body.

"It was barely three days!"

"I know! Still. I'm glad you're back." He kisses me again, and slots his fingers between mine, nudging his glasses back up his nose. "I got a hot tip about a cold treat, we need to hit up the Fleet NEX." I don't even want to admit how much I like being with him. It's back in the usual Fern territory of too much too soon.

Instead of driving we walk over to the Navy Exchange Fleet Store, a small shopping center by the piers. There are groups of sailors everywhere: waiting outside the barber shop, heading into the uniform section, and just loitering outside. I have to drop his hand so we can walk, single file, along the curb to get past a rowdy group of young guys. I make it inside, relishing the cool blast of air conditioning, but when I turn Deacon isn't behind me. I spin in a circle, thinking I had simply missed him, but he's not inside at all. Looking out the front plate glass windows, I see him standing outside the group of guys we had passed. His posture is strange. Tense. Angry. What did I miss? I walk back outside, noticing how Deacon's fists are clenched and his neck looks corded with fury. I stay back, wary of what I could be walking into.

"Calm down, dude, we were just having a little fun!" One guy says. His voice sounds smarmy.

"Seriously! He was joking!" Another guy pipes up.

Deacon is using that borderline scary, steel-laced voice I've heard twice before. "Explain to me how exactly talking about sexually assaulting a female sailor is *just having a little fun?*" It would be a turn on except I'm a little freaked out about what's happening.

"Get real. It wouldn't be forcing her because she'd want it. I mean, look at how she was dressed. She's practically begging for it. You saw her!" The Guy looks around at the group, nodding, like he's looking for support. Everyone else is averting their eyes.

"Of course I saw her, she's here with me." Deacon hasn't raised his voice at all but it's filled with menace and the speaker's face goes white. A smaller guy is nervously tittering over the most vocal guy's shoulder.

"Dude, you probably shouldn't have said her dress would look better on the floor of the fan room." My stomach clenches. I've heard these kinds of jokes before. What woman on a ship hasn't? That's pretty tame honestly.

"What about the part where you said you were going to forcibly drag her in there and, how did you put it again? It was so eloquent." Deacon's muscles are so taut he's vibrating, his shirt stretched tight across his broad back. "Something about making her choke on your cum?"

His words smash into me like a sledgehammer. I bite down on my fear and the bile threatening to rise up in my throat. I have a lot of practice ignoring my own frustrations and hurt. I can deal with this. I imagine myself slapping the guy's face. There would be a loud snapping sound. My palm would be blooming with a stinging heat. His cheek would sport an angry red handprint like a showy advertisement on a billboard, screaming out that something just went down. Except imagining it is all I can do. He isn't worth it. My job is too important to me.

I'm rooted to one spot, trying to get my warring feelings under control, when I see my Chief approaching. He's still in uniform and cuts a commanding presence. He's a teddy bear and want to be with me. I'm sure you have friends and probably had plans, but I'll take whatever you want to give me. No stressing about what comes next. No worrying. Just be together, and we'll take things as they come. Can you do that?" It sounds so reasonable. Why would we do things any other way? Isn't that what dating is supposed to be like? There's no need for me to measure everything against unattainable fairy tale endings. Even if he gets to know me better and decides he's had enough, at least we'll have some good times. And if our brief time together so far is any indication, they will be very good times indeed. One might even argue that I deserve this.

"Let's do it." Both in agreement, we kiss on it. Gah, Deacon can KISS. I want to bottle this up and take it with me so I never forget what it feels like to be completely consumed by him. His lips are like a brand, marking his territory, with toe-curling accuracy.

"Then we're together. I'm not interested in anyone else, I won't be seeing anyone else, and I hope I can expect the same from you."

"Yes."

"As my girl, will you stay with me tonight? Sleep next to me and don't sneak out in the morning?" *Why do I get such a thrill be being called his girl?*

"I'll need to be at the ship at 6 and I don't have a vehicle here."

"I'll take you. We can have breakfast together and I'll drop you off at work." His expression is earnest and cute.

"Very couple-y. You went there pretty quickly."

"I don't want to miss out on anything with you." His words are like a comforting hug.

It's still early so we get redressed and go down to get ice cream. We take it back up to his room and sit out on the balcony. The moonlight is reflecting off of the waves and the breeze carries the scent of the ocean. It would be even more beautiful if there wasn't so much light pollution in Waikiki.

of a man and a good leader. I've learned so much working with him. He doesn't take anyone's shit and has incredibly high expectations for the sailors on our ship.

"Doc, nice to see you away from the chair!" He shakes Deacon's hand and eyes the group suspiciously. "What's going on here?"

I'm finally steady enough to close the space between us and take Deacon's hand, pasting on a smile for the Chief. "I believe it's been sorted out, Chief. How do you know Deacon?"

"Even Chief's need to visit the dentist occasionally." He winks at me, his grin friendly and playful. "EM3 Torres, why do I have a feeling we're going to be having another talk soon?" The smile slides off Chief's face and he glares at The Guy. I'm shocked when I really look at him. I've seen him around the ship. I know who he is. I may have even spoken to him before. It feels like someone is squeezing my intestines.

"It was nothing, Chief."

"Hmm. I guess we'll see. You guys get on out of here." They leave quickly, scattering like cockroaches in the light. When they're gone, Chief turns back to Deacon, his eyes serious. "What do I need to know?"

"I stopped those sailors after hearing them speaking loudly and very explicitly about how they'd choose to sexually assault LTJG McClellan if given the opportunity to trap her in a quiet place alone."

"Who was doing the talking?"

"The one you singled out. Everyone else laughed and egged him on."

"This isn't the first time Torres has done this and talking about an officer, away from the ship, is taking things up a notch. Did you hear this too, Ma'am?"

I shake my head. "Not when he initially said it, but I heard the details repeated." Deacon jerks towards me, tightening his grip on my hand.

"You heard that?" I try to nod but my lip trembles a bit

74

and an angry tear escapes my lashes. I slam my teeth together, biting down on the instinct to shut down. Not here. Not now. "Shit." He envelopes me in a hug, not letting me go as Chief continues.

"I'll speak to his DIVO and we'll go from there."

"I know you need to speak to his Division Officer, but I don't want to be seen as a *problem*, Chief." I have to lift my head to keep my voice from muffling against Deacon's body. "I've heard the stories about harassment and assault reports suddenly changing glowing evals to poor ones. I've worked too hard to be derailed by someone else's words. I'm not letting him fuck with my career."

"*I'm* reporting it." Deacon growls out. "It doesn't matter if she is directly attached to the complaint. You can let me know if you need any more details. I'm happy to answer questions. I'll have Fern text you my number." Chief says his goodbyes and heads into the shops. I'm still standing, my face buried in Deacon's neck. He holds me close, comforting me with his strength and body heat. Kissing the top of my head he murmurs something I can't quite hear. I don't even need the words; I can feel them.

"I didn't hear what he said. You could have kept walking and I would have been none the wiser." I murmur softly.

"But that wouldn't have changed what I heard. What all those guys heard. They're from your ship, Fern. Guys you work with." His tone is still angry. I'm glad it's not directed at me. "I saw them come off the brow. We don't know what they were saying that whole time. Or what they've said in the past. But what happens if it goes unchecked? Does he stick to talking tough in front of the guys? Do we let him think it's okay to demean his coworkers? Or worse, does it escalate?" He swallows loudly, his body tense again. "I don't want to think about what could happen if guys like that are allowed to think that they get a pass. The thought of you, alone on the ship with someone like that…" He squeezes me tighter, pressing his lips to my head again.

"You don't have to worry about me. I can take care of myself if necessary."

"It's not that I think you can't take care of yourself or that you need me to swoop in and rescue you. I know you're strong and capable. I hate the thought that you might *have* to take care of yourself."

I hold him tighter too, hoping to hug some of his anger away. I definitely won't be pointing out that I have had to take care of myself before and I most certainly will again. It's shitty, but that's how the world works when you're a woman, especially a woman working in what has traditionally been a man's world.

"Where are you at, right now?" I relax into him even more, comforted by the question. It's something my therapist asks me and something I ask myself regularly, since I don't have anyone to check in with me. It's nice hearing it from someone else. I appreciate that Deacon is concerned about my feelings after learning about my depression instead of judging me or running the other direction.

"I'm ok. A little shaken, but not sinking lower."

"That's good. You'd tell me if you were, right?"

"Yes. I'd tell you. I'm not really in the mood to go out anymore. I'm sorry if that ruins the night."

"It's on him, not you! And I'm feeling the same way. Let's amend the plan, I think I know what we need."

Deacon picks up a pizza on our way to the hotel and we watch my favorite movie, "Singin' in the Rain." The shock of this afternoon has lessened beneath his care and attention. Deacon reclines against the headboard and pillows, legs stretched out in front of him and I lie back on him. I hold both his hands with our arms crossed over my torso. I feel safe. I tip my head back, kissing the underneath of his chin.

"Thank you for tonight. For standing up for me, and for all of the tangible caring since then. I appreciate you."

"You're welcome," he whispers.

"Deacon?" He looks down into my upturned face, his sharp jaw against mine. "Where are *you* at, right now?"

"It doesn't matter as long as you're good."

I huff, my eyes narrowing. "It does matter. Everyone has feelings, Deacon. Ignoring yours doesn't mean they don't exist. You joked about having braces before. Even more than that, nobody likes a grown man who doesn't understand his own emotions and their importance. *Where are you at?*"

Emerald eyes look past me, unfocused. He exhales loudly. "I don't know. I'm angry, I guess. Filing a report doesn't feel like much and I wish I could do more."

"This is enough." His arms tighten around me and I rest my head back. "You're enough."

Later I doze in his lap and partially wake as he's undressing me and tucking me under the sheet before I slip back into unconsciousness, the heat of his body against my back and his arm draped over my side.

Deacon continues caring for me in his practical, sweet way: sending me off to work with snacks for later, texting goofy GIFs he knows I'll get as soon as I go topside, and showering me with affection. I feel seen for the first time in my life and not only that, but seen and still cared for. It feels like Deacon likes me because of who I am, not in spite of who I am. It's so freeing!

After I stand watch on Friday night I spent some time sitting on the deck so I have cell service. I was invited to go to the North Shore with Norah and her friends. Deacon is coming with me and Brooklyn and Emily are meeting us up there. I got a new swimsuit for the occasion.

I've always been a little indifferent towards my body. There's so much pressure to make yourself appear taller, curvier, longer, or some other things that is opposite of your actual body. Why even try? But Deacon makes me feel sexy as is, so I went shopping for the sole purpose of picking out a swimsuit. Amazingly, it was stress-free! Instead of worrying about fitting the ideal vision of sexy or internalizing all the rules of what I should be looking for to "create the illusion of" whatever strangers think I need to portray to be seen as worthy, I simply picked out what I wanted. I have a bikini. I feel really good in it. It's not particularly skimpy or provocative, just a mossy green that covers what it is supposed to. I love it. I also bought a giant hat that makes me giggle every time I put it on, and an extra tube of sunscreen.

Me: I'm really excited about tomorrow!

Sexy Dentist: Me too! Looking forward to meeting your friends.

Me: You've at least seen Brooklyn & Emily before. That leaves Norah Me: We worked together on my first ship, in Norfolk. Everyone else that's coming are her friends. I've hung out with them once, though, and they all seem cool

Sexy Dentist: I'm also looking forward to seeing you in a swimsuit. How is it that we've only been together IN HAWAI and this has yet to happen?!

Me: Someone keeps taking me back to his room to get naked

Sexy Dentist: That's not all on me. I'm pretty sure the record would show that you ask to go back to the room as often as I do!

Me: That's still your fault, though

Sexy Dentist: How do you figure?

Me: Be less good looking
Me: Don't leave me so satisfied every time
Me: Be unpleasant to be around
Me: Either it's you saying we should go back to the room OR it's you being smoking hot and making me crave your body and causing everyone else to seem boring and dumb in comparison

Sexy Dentist: Damn. I suck.

Me: For sure. You've ruined everything. You've ruined me for other men. You've ruined sex completely. Pretty sure you've ruined friendships too. Way to go, Coleman, you overachiever

Sexy Dentist: I have been told more than once I shouldn't be so focused on achievements. My bad.

Me: You really should be nicer to me

Sexy Dentist: I'll plan on being real nice to you. Tomorrow night.

Me: Promise?

Sexy Dentist: Pinky promise.

Me: Well then, I'll have to be sure to be real nice to you too

8

DEACON

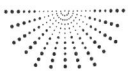

I park at the pier as the sun is peeking over the mountains Saturday morning. As soon as her duty turnover is taken care of, Fern's skipping out to my car, beach bag in hand. She has on a giant fucking hat with a t-shirt dress and she may be the cutest thing I've ever seen. I can't help but laugh as she attempts to climb in. Her hat hits the top of the car, knocking it off of her head, and she's laughing too as she catches it awkwardly and falls into the seat.

"You're adorable." Our kiss lingers, the slow pressure of lips the ideal greeting. "I like your dumb hat."

"Me too," she giggles. "It's so dorky but anything is better than being burned to a crisp by the sun!" She gives me the once over. "Thank goodness you're wearing contacts! I don't need anyone falling for you and trying to steal you away!" I roll my eyes at her, but inside I'm preening.

Norah's group and Fern's other friends are planning on getting there between 8 and 9, but everything I've read says parking around Waimea Bay is awful. I'd rather arrive too early and have extra time with Fern than fight for a parking spot. That shit makes my blood boil. The drive up to the North Shore from Pearl Harbor is a different kind of beautiful. The highway cuts through the hills of Mililani, then we're driving through vast swaths of pineapple fields and Norfolk pine trees, the tall Waianae mountain range to the west until the vast Pacific Ocean opens up before us.

Fern keeps her hand on my leg, filling me in on the latest with the asshole from the Fleet NEX. It seems that her Captain is one of the good ones who is striving to create a work environment that is safe for everyone on board. He takes all harassment very seriously. As this particular guy has had several complaints filed against him and the terrible optics of this time being out in the open, during a huge international exercise where he could have tarnished the image of the US Navy as a whole, no one is taking it lightly. Fern is still hoping she won't have to be officially attached to the report. Of course she knows what a big deal it is, but I understand her feelings. It's not like the military doesn't have a history of brushing off victims, sweeping the problem under the rug and even blaming the victims and penalizing them when they are brave enough to come forward. The whole thing stinks. I'm glad this guy is going to mast over it. Hopefully he learns his lesson.

We circle the small Waimea Bay parking lot four or five times before we spot an older couple crossing the pavement. Thank goodness some people like to get their time in at the beach before breakfast! Fern texts her friends to let them know we're already here and I unload our things. The larger group is supposed to be bringing lunch, so we don't have much to carry. I have a small cooler with drinks and snacks for the two of us and a couple of low beach chairs. Easy. We pick a spot close enough to have a good view of the tall jumping rock, but far enough away that we'll be able to hear ourselves talk. I feel like I'm saying it constantly, like a record that keeps skipping, but the view is incredible. The cerulean and teal water is so clear you can see straight to the bottom. The golden sand slopes down into the gentle crash of the waves and the few people here are so spread out it's as if we have the place to ourselves.

"Did you get us chairs?"

"I know, I said towels would do, but then I worried about it getting too hot. At least this way we're off of the sand a little bit." She smiles knowingly, patting my arm. She has to be biting her tongue, not giving me a hard time when she could. She knew I'd buy chairs, but I swore I wasn't going to spend money on gear just to sit at the beach. "You can say you were right. I probably would have bought a giant fucking canopy to keep you out of the sun if Norah hadn't already said they were bringing a couple!" She laughs, placing a smacking kiss on my cheek.

"Thank you for taking care of me. I don't need to rub it in that I called it because I appreciate that side of you! You're very thoughtful and practical." I've gotta say, it's nice to be appreciated. She digs in her bag, pulling out a container of sunscreen. "I'm going to need your help making sure the back half of my body is covered. And you can't make fun of me when my timer goes off every 90 minutes and I have to reapply. Being a redhead during the summer is no joke! And this is much easier than listening to me whine and applying aloe when I'm as red as a lobster."

She tosses her dress onto the back of her beach chair and I am struggling not to drool all over the place. Why should Fern in a little green bikini be such a big deal? I see her naked all the time! Something is different, though. Some of that timidity is gone. She's not showing off in any way but I can see that she feels good. She's not looking to me for reassurance either. I think that's the sexiest part. She's so comfortable that she doesn't need me to tell her she looks great. I will of course, but she doesn't need to hear it to believe it. I feel a funny, swelling sense of pride. She hands me the sunscreen and I start carefully covering her pale skin, happy that I get to be the one that touches her.

"Is this new?" I ask as I lift the back of her top, making sure she's protected even if her suit shifts. She grins over her shoulder at me.

"I just bought it!"

"You did good, Sweetheart. I don't think anyone has ever looked better in a bikini."

"Thanks, honey."

"Honey? Is that what you landed on?" I smooth my hands down her back, sliding finger tips just inside her suit bottoms.

"I don't know, you called me sweetheart. I thought we were doing a thing."

"I hadn't exactly planned on calling you sweetheart. It felt right, in the moment. Does honey feel right?" She swats my hand playfully as applying sunscreen turns into outright groping her ass.

"Nope." She laughs. "Squirt some sunscreen in my hand so I can work on my front."

"You know, I'd be happy to do all of you." I waggle my eyebrows.

"I'm sure you would." The corner of her mouth quirks up, making me laugh. "But I don't want to get burned waiting for you to finish. You're very," she pauses, giving me a pointed look, "thorough."

"I'll let you do me," I quip, giving her some sunscreen.

"Gladly, dear." She snorts. "Yeah, definitely not using that one either."

We sit and drink the coffee I packed, stretched out in our swanky chairs. Okay, they're nothing fancy, but Fern was right, they're definitely better than the alternative. We're standing up to head into the water when chaos descends on us. First Brooklyn and Emily, laughing loudly and attracting a lot of attention from every guy in the vicinity. Then there's Norah, her housemates, and their neighbors with a trio of adorable curly-headed kids. Like an efficient, beach party machine, they set up a couple of canopies and deposit coolers, chairs, and bags in the shade. They even have a grilling station set up with a small charcoal grill and a prep table. They don't mess around!

I've noticed Fern tends to be more comfortable in one on

one conversations. She sticks to the periphery, observing with a soft smile, responding when spoken to. I feel like I'm more in my element, meeting new people and making friends. The morning slips by with us in the ocean. We float in the waves for a while, everyone taking turns keeping an eye on the kids. Fern and I swim over to the smaller rocks and snorkel. We see schools of brightly colored tropical fish and a giant turtle, drifting around the coral. The beach gets a little more crowded and the local guy who stopped to flirt with Brooklyn recommends that anyone who wants to experience Jump Rock better do it before lunch. Apparently it can get very crowded in the afternoon.

While everyone is debating who is going to jump and when, Brooklyn and the Hawaiian dude go for it. They scale the rock quickly, stopping at the highest point, right in the middle. With a running start he launches off the edge and falls 25 feet down, slicing into the water below. He swims far enough to leave jumping room and yells up to Brooklyn, calling out a loud "chehoo" as she jumps off. She swims to the shore, grinning broadly while the guy goes back to jump again.

"Do you want to jump, Fern?" She looks like she's considering it, maybe a little too seriously. "Do I need to tell you that you couldn't possibly jump off the top?" She smacks me.

"You're not allowed to use that against me, Deacon Coleman!"

"You do that too?" Brooklyn asks with a grin, squeezing the water out of her hair. "She's too easy to manipulate! Fucking with Fernie is my favorite!"

"Wait! You do that on purpose?" Fern mock glares at Brooklyn.

"Of course! Do you think I can be your friend and not know how much you despise being told you can't do something?" I expect Fern to get angry, but she looks lost in thought.

"Jump Rock, Fern?" I ask again.

She stretches slowly, drawing my eyes to her, and then sprints away, calling over her shoulder, "Race you to the top!"

I catch up to her at the base of Jump Rock but her scrabbling skills are impressive. I keep up with my longer reach, barely. There are a few teenagers queued up at the top so we stand behind them, catching our breath and laughing. One kid flips through the air like a legit diver, and the guy after him does an epic cannonball. The dark rock is surprisingly smooth underfoot and the other jumpers have been good about clearing out quickly. Fern peers over the edge, grinning.

"That was a dirty trick." I grouse while she smirks at me. "You know I can't resist looking at you!"

"You liked it." She giggles. She's not wrong. It was hot as hell. "Wanna go together?"

"Let's do it!" I agree.

We take a few steps back, count to three, and leap.

The fall is exhilarating. It feels a lot farther than I expect it to. I'll never forget the weightlessness, the jewel-toned water rushing up to meet us, and the peal of Fern's laughter in my ears as I plunge underneath the blissfully cool waves. I surface to Fern swimming clear of the drop zone, only her head above the water. She's swimming away from the shore and the other people.

"You're going the wrong way!"

"I need a minute,!" She's treading water, her head bobbing comically while she wiggles around.

"What exactly are you doing?"

"The force of the water pushed my top up! I'm trying to fix it but it's twisted and I'm having trouble sorting it out while also not drowning. Dammit!" She groans in frustration. "It's like being trapped in a sweaty, twisted sports bra! You're lucky you don't know that particular brand of hell!"

"Let me help." She made a mess out of it. I try to roll it

down, thinking it might work like the old window shades at Mamaw's house, but give up, holding her steady instead.

"I can't say having your hands on my boobs is helping much." She says wryly. I didn't say *where* I was holding her steady.

"Just covering up the goods. There are children present."

"Uh huh. Why am I not surprised you're copping a feel instead of helping me?"

"I couldn't figure it out. This is more in my wheelhouse. Mamaw always said play to your strengths." She snorts.

"Something tells me I'd like your Mamaw. She sounds like a pistol!"

Sadly, for me, she's able to pull her bikini top over her boobs and I have to slide my hands down to her ribs. Since I already have my hands on her, it's only natural to pull her closer. Cool lips that taste of salt water with a hint of sunscreen meet mine. The timer on her watch goes off, though, and we swim to shore. I can't be the thing that delays sunscreen time.

The guys are grilling and the ladies are setting up the serving area.

"Tacos?" I'm surprised and they look at me like I'm the village idiot. "Where I'm from," I explain, "grilling out means hot dogs and hamburgers. You pack the buns, throw a bag of chips on the table and call it good! I was not expecting to come to the beach and get steak and chicken served up with fire grilled tortillas and what looks like a restaurant's amount of toppings and sides!"

"What can we say? We take our food seriously!" Norah laughs.

Unsurprisingly, lunch is delicious. Everyone scatters afterwards. Some snorkel, some nap in the shade, and some do the brief hike up to the top of the small cliff face off of the beach. Brooklyn is shamelessly flirting with Norah's blond roommate, Ames, but he doesn't seem to be taking the bait. Emily and the dark haired roommate, I think his name is J something, are making the little curly haired girls into sand mermaids. They both seem to be happiest with the kids. Fern stays in her chair, watching the different groups. I wish she wasn't alone. Every time I break off to go over to her I get pulled into another conversation or activity. I keep meaning to check in with her, but never get to it. Everyone here is really cool. I love meeting new people!

By mid-afternoon, we all start packing up to go home. Adults are tired, kids need naps, hell I need a nap at this point! This many hours at the beach really takes it out of you. It's been a full day for sure. It will feel good to get back to the hotel, get cleaned up, and relax in the air conditioning. Maybe I'll pull Fern into the big shower with me, have my way with her, then we can nap naked between the cool sheets.

Fern is subdued on the drive back. For all I know she's merely worn out from the sun and water. But she doesn't seem simply tired. Her hands are clasped together in her lap and she's looking out the window. She feels closed off.

"I had a good time today." I try to pull her out of her thoughts. "They're a pretty fun group. It felt nice making friends."

"I don't really know what that's like. It seemed easy for you, though. I'm glad you got along with everyone. Maybe you'll be able to be a part of the friend group from now on."

"You didn't get along with everyone? Did you not have a good day?"

"It was fine. I had fun at points, the food was good," her half-hearted gesture is indecipherable.

"What's wrong?" The silence stretches out long enough that I think I'll have to ask again when she finally speaks up.

"I just wish I wasn't so awkward. I wanted to talk to Norah more, but she's very social and was busy the whole time. And I know better than to get in the way when Brooklyn and Emily are socializing. I was worried about embarrassing myself in front of people I barely know, and no one really talked to me," she shrugs, her posture dejected.

"I know it's doesn't come naturally, but maybe you could try to meet people halfway? You didn't really make an effort to join in. It can't be everyone else's responsibility to include you."

"You're right," she sighs. "I need to try harder." She frowns, twisting her fingers. "Being with a lot of people, in high energy situations wears me out, mentally, and it's a little disappointing to feel this way, but not have it balanced with the good feelings from fulfilling conversations. I guess I find myself wishing, when I'm in a bigger group, that someone wanted to talk to me as much as I want to talk to them. I always feel like it's one-sided."

"Why can't you just be happy with what you got?"

Fern flinches like I slapped her and her cheeks suddenly look like all her sunscreen applications failed. She's silent, the space between us colder than any air has ever been in Hawai'i.

"I don't like the freeze out. Can you talk to me?" I glance over at her.

"Sorry. I'm trying to sort through what I'm feeling. I'm hurt, but I don't want to lash out. Can I have a few minutes?" I reach across and take her hand in response.

We don't talk as I park, but she also doesn't pull away. We stay physically connected, hands linked, though she feels distant. Guilt settles in my chest, but I'm not even sure what I should be feeling guilty about. Once inside she curls up into an armchair in the corner, her feet tucked up underneath her, a thin finger between her teeth.

"Have you had enough time? We can't deal with this if you won't talk to me."

"I don't want to be something to be *dealt* with, Deacon." Her voice is soft, sad where I thought there'd be anger, cold where I was expecting heat.

"Clearly I made you mad. Are we going to talk about it?"

"I'm not mad." I snort in frustration, dropping down onto the edge of the bed closest to her. She says she's not mad but I'm quickly getting there. "I'm really not mad."

"Then what are you?"

"I'm," she sighs, "sad. Upset. Not angry. I don't want to start a fight."

"You can't spend your life pushing down your hurts and making yourself smaller because you've decided people can't handle it!"

"I didn't just decide that, Deacon. It's been proven. Time and time again." Again, her voice is full of cold dejection, not the fire of frustration. I don't know what to do with that. How do you combat defeat? "The moment I let my guard down, the very second I express something other than the expected surface positivity, I get shut down." She wraps her arms around her knees, looking much younger than she is. It's as if wounded, adolescent Fern has replaced the woman I know. "Whether it's a huge personality flaw or not, I don't deal well with criticism. It wounds me, much deeper than it should, much deeper than anyone realizes. I've always done everything in my power to avoid negative attention. I can't handle it. It was hard at Officer Candidate School, being yelled at and broken down before they built me back up, but I didn't take that to heart. It wasn't about me as a person, it was about the process to become an officer. But when the criticism is aimed at *who I am*? It's awful."

"What does this have to do with—"

She interrupts me with an outstretched hand, her eyes meeting mine for the first time since the beach. The hurt in them makes my lungs stop working for a beat. I did that.

"I let myself be vulnerable with you. Instead of glossing over the day, lying about how wonderful everything was, I told you what I was really feeling, and you criticized me. Even if that is what you needed to say, you could have done it in a better way. You could have been kinder, you could have approached it from the mindset of wanting to know what I was feeling, asking me what I needed. Instead you snapped at me. I've told you more about my past, about my diagnosis and my struggles, than anyone, ever. I trusted you with that,

90

thinking it might help you to understand me better. And yet, knowing all of that, you flippantly chose words that sliced right into the heart of what is wrong with me, what makes me broken and seen as unworthy of affection or friendship. *Why can't you just be happy with what you got?* Why can't I, Deacon? Why can't I just be happy?"

"That's not what I meant, Fern! I wanted you to try as hard as you want other people to. And I hope that you can see, even when you're feeling disappointed, that there was a lot to be happy about today. You're reading too much into this! You're giving my words more weight than you should." *It was one sentence! How can one question cause so many problems?* "How was I supposed to know this would be such a big deal?"

"The fact that you have to ask that is what hurts the most. We've spent all of this time together, time I thought was truly intimate. If you don't know why your opinion of me means so much, then it's hard not to feel like you don't know me at all. Your words will always have more weight. The most weight, the highest ability to maim or heal."

"Why should every small thing I say have so much more pressure on them than other people's words?" I spit out in frustration.

"Because I love you!"

"Say what now?" It pops out. A gut reaction. I wasn't expecting it.

"I love you." She sighs, squeezing her eyes that had widened with that revelation shut tight. "I needed to think through my feelings on today to see that I overreacted. You're right, I was ignoring a lot of good stuff and expecting everyone else to put in more effort than I did. Your snapping at me hurt. It hurts feeling like you don't know me like I thought you did." She stands up, swaying slightly, like a palm in the breeze. "Now that doesn't even matter. Your reaction tells me everything I need to know. I can't believe I did this again." She shakes her head despondently. "I'm sorry. You were clear with what you wanted to get out of these six weeks.

You said you wanted to be free and weren't ready to settle with someone. This is on me. I get attached, I fall too fast, I wish for a real connection so badly that I convince myself it's there when it's not." She crosses her arms, clutching at them like she's holding herself together.

"This is why I pulled away, why I snuck out of your bed. I knew, even after one night, that I would fall for you and get my heart broken. Shit, I even told Brooklyn and Emily, after that first night, that I didn't give you my number because I knew I'd end up falling for someone that saw me as a vacation fuck." That hits me like a knee to the groin and a single tear tracks down her cheek. "Thank you for my first and last summer fling. You were worth every bit of this heartbreak."

She doesn't even say goodbye. She simply walks out. The metallic click of the door falling closed behind her echoes across the silent room. I fall back on the mattress, trying to wrap my brain around what happened. The sheets smell like sex and the sweet combination of white jasmine and mint. Fern. The room is littered with reminders of her: her beach bag that I dropped inside the doorway, the helmet she bought for me to use, a box of protein bars she likes to grab for breakfast. This hasn't really been my room since that first date. It's been ours. Now I have to sleep alone in a bed that smells like Fern's perfume and try to figure out how we got so far from the original plan. This wasn't how things were supposed to go.

❦

9

FERN

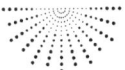

I'm numb, but I'm not worried. This isn't the frozen, grey wasteland of my depression. I still feel like a person, I'm merely a person on hold. The numbness is a gift from my brain instead of a curse; it's a brief respite before the inevitable breakdown. I feel like I'm underwater, my movements slower and strangely fluid. I stand at the curb for a few minutes, lost in thought, before I remember I didn't drive here. I order a ride and wait, trying desperately to keep my brain from looping over the last hour. The more I think about it, the harder it will be to keep the tears at bay.

My driver takes one look at me and turns his music up, giving me space. I've never been more grateful to be ignored. I have him drop me off in the visitor's parking lot outside of the base and I walk through the gate, showing my ID, barely noticing the half mile walk to the ship. I forget to grab dinner before I board. It's Saturday, the kitchen is closed. It's not important enough to leave again. The fact that it's Saturday also means that I have the state room to myself. Another gift.

I strip out of my slightly damp dress and bikini, draping them over my desk to dry. Wrapping up in my robe I grab my towel and shower bag and go to wash the beach off. The hot water takes off some of my chill from the damp clothes, but it can't touch the chill in my bones. I wish I had the luxury of crying in the shower, but this isn't my private space, and it's been ingrained to be frugal with the ship's water. I get cleaned up quickly and take my sorrow back to my room. Only when the door is locked and I'm dry, dressed, and wrapped up in the quiet of my rack do I allow myself to cry. It's too early to go to bed, but my brain doesn't care. I miss the warmth of Deacon's body behind mine, holding me close, making me feel safe and cared for. I lie on my back, pressing the phantom of his touch into the mattress, and fall into a deep, troubled sleep.

The day does not seem brighter when I wake up, but I am resolved regardless. I'm not going to fall into the dark abyss over this. I've already spent too much of my life in the shadow of depression. I've fought too hard to get to where I am today and I'm not going to let myself get derailed so easily. I can be hurt. There's no avoiding that. I *am* hurt. But that is all I'm going to let myself be. So Deacon didn't want my love. That sucks, but it can only break me if I let it. It wasn't his goal to hurt me, and I came out of our time together a better person. I'm better having loved him. I repeat these things throughout the day, reminding myself that I'm stronger than my wounded heart. I don't always believe it, but I'm committed to the idea that the repetition helps. If I hear it enough, it will start to feel true, right?

The week is crawling by. I fill my spare time with extra workouts, turning my overflowing emotions into sweat. Brooklyn and Emily seem to know when to be attentive and when to give me space. I think I may have been wrong about them. Maybe I undervalued our relationship. Things don't seem as one-sided as I thought. Brooklyn jokes to get me smiling and Emily always seems to have a perfectly timed mug of tea or hug for me. That's one more thing my therapist was right about: just because my feelings are very real doesn't make them true. It could be yet another way my broken brain is trying to convince me I'm alone. I wonder what it's like to feel whole and normal? Does anyone actually feel that way?

I was worried about RIMPAC coming to an end. Now I'm ready for it to be over so I can get back to real life. Not that I have anything exciting waiting for me in San Diego, I'm just ready for this island to be my past. John is still coming by the pier, saying hello and lingering awkwardly. Usually I'm busy or with other people so I can avoid him. I don't know what he's up to but I don't really have the mental bandwidth to deal with him right now. With that in mind, I groan out loud as I cross the brow alone and see John walking towards me. His ship isn't even close by, it's not like he happened upon me by accident. That doesn't stop him from clinging to the asinine illusion.

"Oh, hey!" I don't even attempt to hide my eye roll. He might as well have thrown in an in-genuine *fancy meeting you here*. "How's it going, Snaggletooth?"

"For the last time, please stop calling me that, John. Why are you here?"

"It's just a nickname, Fern. You don't have to be so sensitive."

"I AM sensitive. That's me. And you know this. So your willful choice to be *insensitive* is pissing me off. This is not a me problem, it's a you problem." I remember what Deacon said about him and I'm frustrated and sad all at once. "I'm tired of being made fun of and I have somewhere to be."

"I wasn't making fun, Fern! I like your snaggletooth." He looks like a chastised child, pouting at me.

"How was I supposed to know something you've never said? You've always used it as a joke and it makes me feel self-conscious. Picking at me and poking fun at my insecurities is not flirting, John, and it never has been." I try to push past him and he grabs onto my wrist, spinning me back towards him.

"I'm sorry. Can we please talk?"

"We don't have any reason to talk. We're not friends. You dumped me over a year ago and nothing has changed."

"Maybe I missed you. Maybe I wondered if we could try things again, in California."

"No." I pull my wrist gently from his hand and start down the stairs. It takes a few seconds before John starts following me.

"Wait, what?"

"I know my being decisive must be confusing for you but my answer is no. I don't need anyone's *maybes*. I'm not a back-up plan or a body to fill the lonely time until someone better comes along. So, in short, no. We dated, it ended, I don't want to go back." He's still following me but he's stopped talking and I stop walking, momentarily frozen by the sight of Deacon standing at the foot of the stairs. The green of his shirt makes his eyes brighter and his smile still makes my knees weak. He looks behind me, seeing John and his face goes from a nervous smile to angry. That change gets me walking again. I've had enough drama for one afternoon, thank you very much.

"Why the fuck is he here?" Deacon growls.

"I could ask the same of you. Why are you here, Deacon?" I brush past him, continuing on my original mission: to get one of those local ice cream sandwiches everyone has been talking about. I'm only on Oʻahu for a few more days and I still haven't had one of Uncle's treats.

"Fern!" His steps pick up behind me and once again I'm grabbed and spun around. "Please don't get back with him! He doesn't deserve you! You can't choose someone that doesn't even think to tell you what he likes about you!"

Fuck, this hurts. "He's not you." I almost whisper. He looks as hurt as I feel. That's not comforting. I don't want him to hurt. "This isn't a competition. There are no winners here. Just guys that didn't want what I was offering. John was leaving. We have nothing to talk about and I had to remind him of that. And now I'm leaving too." I turn towards the road again but only make it two steps before I'm stopped again.

"Please, Fern, wait?" My frustrations bubble over and in a rarely seen phenomena, I explode.

"Dammit! All I wanted was an ice cream sandwich! I don't want to explain to my ex that I don't like being belittled and have no interest in being his relationship seat filler! And I don't know why you're suddenly here, but I can't take anymore." I stifle a sob and press on. "I don't want to keep hurting. I don't want to cry. I just want some fucking ice cream between two giant cookies! Is that too much to ask?! Can't I have *one* thing I want?"

Deacon reaches towards me, then stops, like he thinks better of touching me. I'm glad. I can't handle the memory of his hands on me, I don't want the reality when it's not the way I want. "I told you I loved you, Deacon!" I hate the way my voice breaks. I sound weak. "And you stared at me like I had ruined what we had. This is like John all over again. I know, I'm not worth the effort. Not to John and not to you. Here's the problem, though," I straighten up, giving myself permission to really look at him one last time. He is so handsome I ache. "I may not be worth it to you, but my time with you helped me to see that I am not unworthy. I'm not settling. It's not enough anymore. I don't want whatever scraps someone is willing to give me. I want it all, and I want it with someone who isn't afraid of how much I feel. I'm tired of apologizing for who I am." The tears are falling, unbidden, and I scrub them away with a careless swipe of the back of my hand. "If you'll excuse me, I'm going to find my dessert. All this crying without ice cream is bullshit."

I turn back, my energy depleted, and start to trudge towards the Fleet NEX. A dark shape rushes past me and I realize it's Deacon, sprinting across the road. This whole thing has been so weird, I don't have it in me to ask what is going on. Why shouldn't he literally run away from me? I'm now repelling people, but more dynamically. I chuckle bitterly at that and keep walking, hands thrust into my shorts pockets. I'll have my ice cream and go back to my rack. Sleep would be a welcome break from today. I reach the sidewalk, the same place where Deacon confronted that group of young sailors, and he's running out of the door of the shop, towards me, a plastic package in his hand. He thrusts it towards me, out of breath.

"Here. It's lilikoi ice cream on sugar cookies. I heard it's the best one." He leans forward, breathing deeply. "Now please, can I say something?"

I lift one shoulder in a shrug, opening my ice cream sandwich. Why did he do this? I have to let the hot summer air warm it up a little so it's soft enough to bite into. I concentrate on my dessert, not wanting the pain that comes from looking into his emerald eyes.

"Fern, you're wrong." My head jerks up automatically. How dare he? He keeps talking before I can get a word in edgewise. "I do think you're worth it. You're more than worth the effort it would take to overcome an ocean between us. But you were right, when you told me that—" he takes a deep breath and pushes his glasses back up to the bridge of his nose with one knuckle. "When you told me you loved me, I wasn't ready for it. You did ruin what we had. It was too superficial. My plan for hanging out for six weeks couldn't support the weight of your confession."

I try to take a bite of the ice cream sandwich but the cookies are still too hard and it tastes like ash in my mouth anyway. "I really didn't need you to confirm my fears, Deacon. It already hurts enough without that."

"No, Sweetheart, you're misunderstanding me." He steps closer, bringing his large, warm hand up to cradle my cheek. It takes everything in me not to lean into his touch. "I'm sorry for my lack of a reaction. I'm not very good with feelings, but you help me with that and make me want to try harder, to be better. I think we need to ditch the plan. Having fun for six weeks isn't enough. Not with you. I love you, Fern McClellan, and I'll take whatever you'll give me: the nights you have left on island, phone calls, video chats, visits, vacations, maneuvering orders to be together." He pauses to lean forward and press his lips to my forehead. "I'll do whatever it takes to keep you in my life. If you want that." He looks at me expectantly and the uncertainty in his eyes does me in. I burrow into his firm chest, wrapping my arms around him. I'm crying again but I can't help it and this time I don't mind.

"You love me?" I tip my head back to look at him, my hurts soothed by his words and the balm of his presence.

"I love you." He kisses me and, like the first time, I feel incandescent. I've missed this. His touch is soft, at first, and then his hands slide up, tangling in my hair and angling my face as the kiss deepens. It's like that first sip of ice cold water after a hard workout. I'm drinking him in and it only makes me want more.

"Your ice cream is melting!" Someone yells behind us, laughing.

"I'll get you another one," Deacon murmurs, between soft kisses.

"I think it's dripping on your clothes."

"Then we'll need to take them off." I giggle against him and he presses a final, firm kiss on my lips. "Are you laughing because you're going to ask what I think you're going to ask?" I smile, my heart lifted and my hurts gone as I look into the face of the man I love.

"Can we go back to your room?"

EPILOGUE

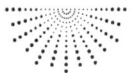

A MONTH LATER - DEACON

I'm putting the finishing touches on dinner when I hear the front door open. I tend to take care of the evening meals since my schedule doesn't vary much. Arms wrap around me from behind and I put down the spoon, turning so I can hold her properly. Her long red hair is in a regulation bun and she's still in uniform, but Fern is always the most beautiful woman I've ever seen. I press a kiss into the top of her head as she leans into me wearily.

"Long day?" She groans in response.

"It was ok, just a lot to do to get ready for the training exercise." She tips her face up for a kiss. "It smells good in here. I'm gonna get changed before we eat."

"Want me to watch?" She rolls her eyes at me.

"If you come back to our bedroom we won't eat and I'm starving!"

"Oh, I'll eat..." I wiggle my eyebrows at her.

She snorts, pushing away from me. "Later, Deacon. I love you, but I need food." I love messing with her.

While Fern changes out of her uniform, I set the table. I still can't wrap my brain around our whiplash quick change of circumstances. She was only gone a week before she was sent back here TAD. Basically that's a temporary duty. She's helping out with a training exercise. It gets better though. An old shipmate is Fern's detailer. She just got word that the guy who was set to be the aide for the admiral at MIDPAC got a DUI and they reconsidered her nomination. Instead of staying in San Diego, Fern is taking a hot fill position here! We went from thinking we'd have to figure out dating long distance to living together in the span of two weeks. Honestly, that's pretty on brand for us.

I love our apartment. It's perfect for us and Fern's stuff isn't even here yet. Even without her belongings, she's still managed to make it feel like a home instead of a one bedroom apartment. It's cozy, bright, and in the heart of cool Kaka'ako. Our commute is easy and we're close to good food and beaches. None of that's important though. I'd live in a cardboard box if Fern was with me. She pokes her head out of the bedroom door.

"Today *is* Thursday, right?" Her eyes are narrowed at me.

"It is. I can't believe I forgot!"

"You had me all confused! I thought I must have had the day wrong otherwise why would you be fully dressed?! Ditch the clothes, Coleman, it's Thirsty Thursday!" She pads out in my favorite "outfit" of hers: a so-thin-it's-almost-sheer tank top and a thong. Thursdays are the best. I make dinner and we eat in our underwear. Why? No reason other than I look for any excuse to get Fern as close to naked as possible. I still can't get enough of her. I'm sure I never will.

We eat and talk about anything but our work days. We have to be intentional about it or our life is all Navy all the time. I'm soaking up this time with her in particular because as soon as she moves here for real, she'll be traveling quite a bit for her new job. Admiral's have very demanding schedules. It will work out though, because she'll come home to me. She *is* home to me.

It's like I have a front row seat to Fern blossoming. She's

working incredibly hard, both on her career and on herself. I'm so proud of her. She's more confident and assured and she helps me stay connected and vulnerable with her. I have to really work at it as—it definitely doesn't come naturally—but she's more than worth the effort. She needs that depth of feeling and I'd do just about anything to make her happy.

"I haven't heard from Daisy in a couple of days, is she doing ok?" Fern asks as she clears our dishes off the table. I join her at the sink, rinsing what she washes. I never would have thought I'd like having a domestic routine with someone, but I really do. Everything is better with a true partner. Who knew?

"She's busy with work. But she's talking about coming out here, so we may be seeing her soon." Fern and my sister get along really well. She talks to her as much as I do, sometimes more. Daisy says they're besties. That word is ridiculous but I dig the sentiment. My two favorite women became quick best friends.

"How soon? What's she thinking?" Fern leans against the counter, the long lines of her body on display. TGIT.

"Well, that depends mostly on you."

Here we go. I've been preparing, planning, waiting impatiently for this moment and now that it's here I feel like my heart is trying to force it's way up into my throat. Fuck, I'm nervous. My palms are sweating and I try to sneakily wipe them on the back of my boxer briefs.

"Why? Does she need my schedule to plan around or something? I could probably take some leave with enough warning."

"Well, she for sure wants to be here for the wedding." She freezes, eyes wide. "I think she's hoping to be up there with you, truth be told. So the questions are: do you want to do it here and how long are you going to make me wait?"

I'll be honest, I was hoping she'd jump me. Some contact, maybe getting to hold her in my arms, kissing. Anything to indicate she wants this as much as I do. Instead, she simply stands there. Then she crosses her arms over her chest and tips her head, staring me down. *What is happening here?*

"Shit!" I realize the problem. "Wait here! I wasn't counting on Thirsty Thursday!" I jog back to the bedroom, dig in the pocket of my discarded shorts, and pull out the ring box. I can't believe I forgot the ring! Nervous idiot. I hurry back out to her. She's still standing the same way, a curtain of red waves falling over one shoulder.

"Sorry! I forgot this part. Here." I hand her the open ring box. I obsessed over the ring, wanting to find the perfect, unique piece of jewelry to show Fern how much I love her. There are curling, delicate hapuʻu ferns in gold with tiny diamonds dotting their ends. They meet in the middle to support a round emerald. She's staring at it intently, running a fingertip over the band. I find myself rambling, trying to fill the silence I wasn't expecting to be there.

"Those are Hawaiian ferns. And, uh, an emerald. You're too special for a basic diamond…" My voice trails off. "Fern? You're not really saying anything. I guess I thought you'd have a response to me saying I want to spend my life with you." She finally looks up at me and her expression surprises me. There's mischief in her eyes.

"Except you didn't."

"I didn't what?"

"You didn't say you wanted to spend your life with me. Actually, if we're arguing details, you didn't exactly ask me the most important question either. I mean, I know you're a very practical guy and romance isn't your native tongue, but was *this* the big gesture, Deacon? Asking how long I'd make you wait? In our kitchen? In our underwear?" She's barely containing her grin now. I grab her, wrapping my arms around her and pulling her against me. She giggles, her arms and the ring box trapped between us.

"Fine, you're right. I didn't think about the romance angle.

You deserve romance, Fern, you really do. But all I could think about was how much I want to be with you. Forever. I wanted you to have the perfect ring. I wanted to start planning our wedding and navigate orders as a mil-to-mil couple. I forgot about the grand gesture. Hell, I forgot to ask! That's how much I love you. That's how much I want to be with you. I forget myself. I lose all reason."

"That's pretty fucking romantic, Deacon." She slides her arms out from between us and over my shoulders, bringing her lips to mine. This dance of tongues, the sliding of lips, the pressing of our bodies is as exciting as it is familiar. My stomach is still a mass of knotted up nerves. I want this so badly. I've never wanted anything so much. Fern puts her hands on my face and there's a cold spot on my right cheek. I pull her hand away, seeing the ring on her finger.

"It looks good, right?" She grins, holding her hand out and spreading her fingers to display it better.

"Are we doing this? Is that a yes? You didn't actually say."

"And you didn't actually ask so I figured this was fine." I slap her ass and she squeals, jumping out of my arms.

"I can't decide if I want to strangle you or fuck you senseless." She's backing away even as I step forward.

"I know which one I'd choose." She turns and runs to the bedroom, making it through the door before I catch her, grabbing her from behind and picking her up before tossing her onto the bed. I cover her with my body, trapping her as she laughs. "I love you, Deacon."

"Forever?" Her face grows serious.

"Forever." She kisses me softly, sweetly. "Always." I want her in a deeper, more possessive way than I ever have. Like I want to mark her as mine. The urge is primitive and automatic.

"I want to see my ring on you."

"You have!" She wiggles her fingers on her left hand.

"*Only* my ring." Her skin flushes my favorite shade of pink.

I like to think of it as *arousal pink*. I stand up, pushing down my underwear before sliding hers down her legs. I climb over her, kissing my way up her body. She pulls her top off, tossing it away as I reach the apex of her legs. I slide my fingers through her silky folds, following with my tongue.

"Only this until I die? How did I get so lucky?"

"Don't stop! I'm not going to last long." I look up, flicking her clit with my tongue and she's watching me, sucking on her bottom lip. I lick and lap, drunk off the taste of her, turned on by the way she's watching. "Thirsty Thursdays are good foreplay."

Her head falls back on the mattress as I suck her into my mouth. She lifts up, muscles tightening. I run a finger down, under my mouth, stroking lightly, and she strains higher before crying out and collapsing onto the bed. Orgasms don't make Fern tired, they're like a shot of adrenaline. She's relaxed now but I know her body better than my own. She's going to want more and my dick can't wait to give it to her. I stand and Fern sits up, pointing at the top of the bed.

"Sit."

"I like when you're bossy." I sit, leaning against the headboard and she crawls over, climbing into my lap. Her hair falls over her shoulders in wild waves and I brush them back from her face. Her big green eyes are shining. "You're so beautiful. I can't tell you how glad I am you went to karaoke with Brooklyn and Emily. Where would I be if you hadn't?"

"Here. With me. I would have ended up in your chair or we would have run into each other in the lobby of the hotel. It was meant to be. We would have found each other. I'm sure of it."

She slides forward, rubbing her arousal down my shaft. She raises herself up, aligning my head with her center, and lowers herself down. There's nothing between us. She wraps her arms and legs around me, holding me close, and I kiss her deeply. We move as one until it's hard to tell where I end and she begins. She's squeezing me with her inner muscles every time she raises up and rotating her hips when she comes down and it feels unreal. Fucking amazing. There's something deeper happening here, beyond the mere joining of our bodies. I'm running my hands over every inch of skin I can reach and she's wrapped around me, hands in my hair, body pressed as close as can be. Every nerve ending is alight and I can feel my release gathering low, the heat pooling between us. Fern's movements have sped up and she's jerking at the end of every stroke, barely restrained. She's right there too. She licks down my neck, biting the spot that she knows gets me.

"Let go. Come with me." She grazes with her teeth, biting again and I explode into her, growling and clutching her to me. She rises one last time, whole body tensing before she drops her head back, gasping and shaking. I lie her back and slide down next to her, mess be damned. She scoots up against me, chest to chest, tucking her head in the spot that feels like it was made for her. My fiancee presses her lips to my chest, over my heart. Her heart, really. She's the only one it has ever truly belonged to.

"I love you. Let's not wait too long to get married. Winter would be nice." Her lips brush my skin with every word.

"Whatever you want, Sweetheart. As long as you're the one saying you will, the rest is only details."

"I agree. I don't want too much fuss, Deacon. Just you."

I hold her, her heart beating next to mine. I'm sure we'll have our share of challenges in our future. It won't be easy to juggle two military careers with demanding schedules. Still, there's no one else I'd rather do it with. I had no inkling, when I moved to paradise, how much my life was going to change. I figured on career advancement, hoped I'd make some friends, and planned on exploring the island while it was home. Who knew one night in Waikiki would change all of that. One night and one girl. My girl. My whole heart, everything I ever wanted and a thousand things I didn't even know I needed, all in one emotional, deep, driven, awkward and hilarious, red headed naval officer. My Fern.

Did you love this introduction to the Oahu Naval Officers Series? Are you ready to meet the next officer headed to an unexpected happily ever after? Read ahead to get a glimpse of Norah's very own Hawaiian love story!

NORAH

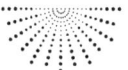

Frankly, I cannot believe what I'm hearing. My little Fern. Shy, funny, often unsure of herself, awkward Fern is engaged! How does that even happen? She was here 2 weeks less than I've been, and only temporarily! I guess when you fall in love... I don't even know how to finish that sentence. I mean, I like people, but I'll never understand feelings. Fern is all about the feelings so I suppose it makes sense that she would be in this position now. I'm happy for her. Deacon is a good guy and he actually values who she is, unlike the last asshat she dated. Oh shit, I hope there's karaoke at their reception! That would be so fun. Seeing them together gives me a twinge of loneliness. That's not in my future, though. I'm here for one thing: the job.

Hawai'i is beautiful, no doubt. I hope to see and experience as much as I can while I'm here. I don't want to waste this opportunity. But I'm also going to work on building up my savings, put on Lieutenant, and be the best Surface Warfare Naval Officer I can be. A relationship is not anywhere near that list. Not that I have a queue of interested parties. That is definitely not one of my problems. Nor is a lack of self-confidence. I *am* the issue, though. I may be tall, blonde and in fantastic shape (*what? I love exercise, it makes me feel clearheaded!*) but I'm also successful, ambitious, work in a male dominated field and make good money. I'm intimidating as fuck. Can you imagine the type of guy it would take to be my match? Pretty sure he doesn't exist.

PLAYLIST

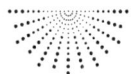

"Don't You Want Me" - The Human League
"Adore You" - Harry Styles
"Bloom" - Troye Sivan
"Fire for You" - Cannons
"Can I Call You Tonight?" - Dayglow
"Are You Bored Yet?" - Wallows ft Clairo
"Shaka & Shine" - Keilana

ACKNOWLEDGMENTS

A million thanks to my sisters, Tessa and D'dee, for being my first readers and biggest cheerleaders. Even when life is crazy busy, you always make time for me. Love you forever, sissies!

Big thanks to my beta readers and fellow romance authors, Jess Mastorakos and Rietta Boksha! You two are awesome! I hope you know how much appreciate your patience with this baby author's mountains of questions.

Kelly Helmick of Dog Star Creative Co Editing, you are my new favorite person! I can't believe I lucked out on having such an incredible beta reader, editor and all around amazing human from a Facebook group post! Thank you for your guidance, gentle critiques and laughs! I can't wait to work with you again.

Thank you to the awesome staff at Wang Chung's for answering my questions about how things were before COVID changed how restaurants and bars can operate on Oʻahu. Even with the new changes, we had so much fun there!

Of course my family deserve all the praise for putting up with my hyper-focus while I'm writing, late dinners, and distracted conversations. But they won't be reading this so they'll get their thanks in person, as it should be.

And if you've made it this far, dear reader, THANK YOU! Thank you for joining me on this journey!

Keep an eye out for "Like a Good Neighbor," coming soon!

ABOUT THE AUTHOR

Drea lives on the beautiful island of Oʻahu, Hawaiʻi with her Sailor and 5 kids. She drinks a lot of coffee, reads a lot of books, and has a lot of tattoos. As a neurodivergent author, her dream characters and scenarios involve complex people, emotional wounds, normalizing nurturing those things that make us unique, and the magic of finding the person who sees all of you and still wants more.
When not writing, she can be found weightlifting with her sailor, avoiding social engagements, and singing and playing guitar (alongside that handsome sailor) with their church worship band.

Follow Drea on:
Website: http://www.dreabraddock.com
Facebook: www.facebook.com/groups/hanamaucollective
Instagram: www.instagram.com/author.drea.braddock
Twitter: www.twitter.com/authordrea

Made in the USA
Middletown, DE
22 July 2022

69897349R00066